Adam's Eve

Adam's Eve

Eric Lee

2003

Adam's Eve

At the time I began this story I didn't consider myself a writer, but the inspiration struck me so feverently that I was left with no choice but to write it down and share it with the world. May God continue to bless me with the excitement, skill and perseverance that it will take to present this as my gift to all that will be helped by it.

I am dedicating this story to my brother. To Jarrell and Vicki and their daughters Nicole, Brittany and Brieanne who first demonstrated to me the beauty and purity of interracial love. To my mom and dad who brought me back to the planet and offered me the most wonderful love any child could ask. Finally, but by no means least importantly to my perfect little girl Erica and her beautiful little brothers Forrest and Justin who illustrate to me daily how precious God meant life to be. How love only creates perfection and peace in all children, in spite of any perceived differences, racial or otherwise.

My deepest heartfelt love and appreciation goes out to all of you. I hope that this story that I share comes close to the gift that you have given me in the form of your constant examples that God is alive at every moment in each and every last one of us. I love you!

1.

The pilot's voice rang over the radio, "This is Piper 7143 Alpha Lima. I am experiencing difficulties. Is there anyone listening that can verify my transmission?"

Adam repeated the request, but again there was no reply. It was a lonely feeling up there at 10,000 feet, especially on this ominous evening. Except for the flashes of lightning, the night was pitch black. This thunderstorm was among the worst he had experienced since his flight training. He fought the wind and turbulence as they tossed his nimble, single-engine aircraft like a yacht in stormy seas.

He again tried the radio, only to hear the static of the airwaves and the crackling of electricity in the air. Adam, a well-trained pilot, remained cool and searched for a solution.

Lightning steadily lit up around him and thunder rocked the plane. Adam tried the radio one last time—it was dead. He quickly adjusted his course to 295 degrees, the last instruction received from air traffic control before his radio went out.

He contemplated an emergency landing as his plane slowly descended. Visibility outside was down to roughly a hundred feet. There was no way of knowing if other aircraft or radio towers were in the vicinity. He made an attempt to calculate his location by the amount of time he had flown since his last contact with air traffic control. He looked at his storm scope and tried to get a reading of the wind direction and velocity, but there was no real way of determining how accurately the scope was actually receiving storm cell signals. Adam's calculations would be highly technical guesswork.

Time was critical. Adam had to set up his plan of action before fuel also became an issue. He set his transponder frequency on 7700, the standard setting for aircraft emergencies. He wondered if the transponder was in fact transmitting, or if it was dead like all of his other equipment. He again tried the radio to see if he could get a response.

"This is Malibu 7143 Alpha Lima. I am experiencing technical difficulties. Mayday, Mayday, Mayday! Is there anyone out there who can hear me?"

He began to despair, and wondered if this would be the last flight in his improbable piloting career. He stilled his mind, realizing his only chance to pull through this precarious situation was to stay calm and believe he could make it. He began to execute his descent.

He banked the aircraft 30 degrees, enough to give him a standard turn for a slow, controlled, spiral descent. He brought the power way back and added full flaps to safely hasten the process. His plan was to get down to 3,500 feet so he could identify the land beneath him. If so, he could locate a place to put his plane down, possibly an airport.

Just as Adam began to feel in control, the airplane rocked violently as lightning struck in front of the small craft. The lights went out briefly and fear gripped him. This was not the type of experience Adam had wanted on the way to changing the rest of his life. This trip to the Northwest was to be smooth sailing, as would his purchase of the small airport at Friday Harbor. Now he just wondered if he would make it through the night. As he continued, Adam heard the dreaded knock of the plane's engine. Either the fuel was getting dangerously low or it was out altogether. A few seconds later, the engine went completely dead.

The situation had become very simple for Adam. He no longer had to think and make hard decisions, for at this point most of his choices were gone. His focus became crystal clear since his radio, his course, and remaining fuel were no longer issues. His only concern was saving his own life.

Adam felt a surge of energy that he had never experienced before. If there was in fact a God, this is what it felt like to communicate directly with Her spirit. Adam flashed a look outside of the cockpit window. Down below he could see a small cluster of lights that looked to be a small town. As he descended, the cluster of lights grew near faster than he was trained to allow. His airspeed had become dangerously high. Adam quickly set his automatic pilot trim-tabs to maximize his glide ratio and slowed his descent to a speed that would allow him to make a safe landing.

He banked left and turned away from the town's lights, then checked his airspeed. It was at 95 knots, right where it should be. He was now at 2,000 feet and descending. He probably had two to three minutes to find an area that was suitable for landing. Adam quickly determined the wind direction and set up an approach. These tasks were usually routine, but obviously this night held unusual circumstances. He still couldn't see the surface well enough to avoid power lines and trees.

Another lightning bolt struck directly beside the sleek aircraft. The plane tilted with the force of it, but the only damage done was the loss of precious seconds ticking away as Adam tried to gather himself and focus on the ground below. Desperately, he tried to find a safe clearing to land his prized possession. He saw what he thought was an opening off his right shoulder, so he quickly turned the yoke and banked a 45-degree turn.

Just as he lined himself up with the clearing, the craft abruptly hit the ground. As Adam realized what was happening, his head was thrashed sideways and slammed against the pilot's side window.

2.

The old man sat at a rickety table, eating a ham and cheese sandwich on bread a couple days beyond fresh. Nevertheless, he was enjoying the meal as he sipped on black tea. Sam had learned to enjoy the simple pleasures of his own company, never really having been accepted in the small, southern community on whose outskirts he resided. His only motivation for staying was the 240-acre plot he occupied left to him by a relative in the 1950s.

As he sat there alone, his mind began to wander. Today his thoughts took him to his childhood and a snapshot of playing in the streets of St. Paul, Minnesota. Sam's home life had been tumultuous, frequently defined by the violent abuse of his father, Henry. It was not uncommon to be jolted out of his sleep, either the direct recipient of the physical abuse or as witness to abuse against, Florence, his mother.

These times would have gone on indefinitely if it were not for Henry being murdered in an alley one night. He had picked a fight with the wrong person. It seems the time always came when anger led to one's ultimate undoing. For Henry it came in the form of four bullets to the head. The man who would not abide his belligerence was Willie Smith, a gangster from Kansas City. Willie had blown into town to lay low because things had gotten a little hot for him in "KC." He had planned to let things cool down in St. Paul, but instead brought the heat back down on himself by shooting Henry. Rumor had it he pushed on to Gary, Indiana and was never heard from again.

Henry's death was bittersweet for Florence and ten-year-old Sam. Often they had wished him dead, but when he was gone they had to deal with the financial realities of being a single-parent household in the 1930s. Even with the help of Florence's mother, who let them stay in her home, Florence found herself working two menial jobs to make ends meet.

Things seemed to be okay, until Florence fell in love with a Negro hustler named George White. George had come to her rescue one day when he came upon a group of hoodlums hassling her as she walked home from the market. After scattering the youths, George offered to carry her bags. At first she resisted, but the smooth-talking George convinced her she would be much safer in his presence. In the coming weeks, George made a point to rendezvous with Florence at the same spot, always welcomed by George's wide grin framed by his milk chocolate complexion. He would assist her carrying her things, assure that she arrived safely home. In that time, what had been a casual acquaintance had given rise to full-blown romance. Florence had been unaccustomed to such benevolence from a man, and as she began to trust its genuineness she found herself yielding to her own feelings of tenderness.

George White was incredibly generous. He had grown up on the street and had never forgotten the charity of a few kind strangers. He was known for doing things like giving his last thirty dollars to a woman on the street with her two children. In some circles, such acts would be termed philanthropy, but on the streets of a small, racist community, he was seen as nothing more than a streetwise, Negro numbers runner.

For some time, Florence and George were able to keep their relationship under cover, but as their feelings deepened it became more challenging. The passion in their glances was unmistakable to anyone who was paying attention. Florence realized this was the love she had waited for all her life and she could hardly bear stifling it. George found himself having to create excuses in order to stop by. On each of these occasions he came bearing gifts for the lovely Florence and Sam. It reached a point where George was providing in gifts more than Florence was making at her two jobs combined. Sometimes it was in the form of food, rides, or occasionally cash. But it wasn't the gifts Florence wanted. As nice as they were, she felt she had to refuse, especially the cash. George always managed to find a way to leave them for her nonetheless.

Underlying the outward actions meant to draw judgmental eyes away was the immense love the two shared. There was no question in either of their minds that this was the reason for being together. As painful as it was, they also knew it would never work if openly acknowledged. Neither one of their races would support such a relationship. It was simply out of the question.

It was the pain of their unexpressed desire that ultimately broke them apart. This was a love to be announced to the world, to be held up as an expression of the ultimate joy of what it is to be human. To sequester it away and hold it in darkness was to be denied life. They became reckless and began publicly displaying their affection toward each other. They were seen together more frequently, until those with small minds who live in hateful boxes would tolerate no more. When Florence and George were not deterred by the persistent harassment, a group of racist vigilantes took it upon themselves to run George out of town.

After George moved on, Florence was left to withstand the taunts and jeers of being called a "nigger-loving slut." It was a difficult time for Sam, as he innocently watched the pain his beautiful mother experienced from two sides—the abuse from spiteful people in the community and the even greater pain of losing the only man who had ever truly loved her.

The remainder of Sam's childhood was a living hell. The shame of his mom's forbidden romance followed them for the next decade. All through school he was tortured as the son of a "nigger lover." In the evening he would return home to his mother's despair, until one day she snapped. She could no longer endure the pain of a life lived without love, both from George and those around her whose only purpose seemed to be to hate. She was found dead in her bedroom from an overdose of sleeping pills. No note was left, but then none was really needed. So lost in her own pain, she hadn't stopped to think that she had left Sam a legacy of alienation and emptiness. It had been the saddest day of Sam's young life.

At eighteen, Sam had a bitter resentment towards life, especially Negroes, having blamed George for his ultimate despair. World War II was in full swing by then, and Sam saw an opportunity to unleash some of the immense anger bottled up inside himself. Germany was the perfect target, representing ultimate evil which must be subdued.

After boot camp, Sam found himself in the thick of one of history's greatest wars. Hitler was making a fast break across Europe, and it appeared as though tyranny would dominate the foreseeable future. Sam was stationed in Italy and quickly found in the Nazis an ample target at which to aim his rage.

One afternoon while on routine patrol, his squadron was surrounded. All around him Sam saw his squad being slaughtered by exploding bombs and a barrage of bullets. Never had he experienced or even imagined such carnage. A small group of the men began running as fast as they could in retreat. As they made their way through the forest, their numbers continued to drop under the relentless Nazi attack. Sam was among those running for their lives. When he reached a clearing at the edge of the forest, he was suddenly aware that no one else had made it to this point with him. He was all alone, with the exception of the German troops who would not cease their assault until all American soldiers were terminated.

Suddenly, Sam went thrashing to the ground from the force of an explosion. There was no time to waste in pulling himself together and finding cover. As he tried to move he felt a hot, burning pain coursing through his right leg.

"Oh my God!" Sam gasped as he looked down to see a six-inch-long, two-inch-deep gash that had laid open his right thigh. He experienced the uncomfortable vulnerability of feeling the warm air blowing against his exposed flesh as blood continued flowing from his open wound.

As he lay helpless in the clearing he heard the thunderous roar of aircraft engines. He shifted his sight to the sky above, feeling a surge of hope as he noted the "Made in America" signature on the two P-51 Mustangs. It felt as though he were witnessing God.

The U.S. fighters pounded the German infantry with .90-mm fire and half-ton bombs until they pushed them back into the forest. Sam heaved a deep sigh of relief when he saw the enemy retreat behind the trees. He also realized it would only be a matter of time after the fighters left before the Nazis would return to finish the massacre.

Then Sam watched as one of the P-51s circled back. The fighter was headed directly toward the clearing. The aircraft suddenly went silent, as if the power had been shut off.

The P-51 was in a steep-angled and rapid descent, heading straight for him. The craft had been shot down. Sam's distracted amazement quickly turned to terror as the rifle fire resumed from the enemy troops camouflaged in the forest. He could see silhouettes of German soldiers wading out from behind the trees. As the P-51 grew closer, the ground fire intensified.

Sam reached for his rifle. If it was his time to die, he was going to go down with pride, fighting like a soldier. He started shooting at the enemy in the distance as the P-51 whizzed over his head. Shooting like there was no tomorrow, Sam released his grief for the brave pilot who was willing to crash in an attempt to save him.

Sam, so blinded by his own rage the adrenaline driving him to rally in the fight for his life, hadn't noticed the perfectly-executed, soft-field landing performed by the pilot of the beautiful P-51 Mustang. He did, however, notice when the aircraft's engine re-fired. With a quick glance over his shoulder, he saw the P-51 taxiing toward him. He was astonished and tried to get up, but fell back to the ground, grimacing in pain. The pilot nosed his plane towards the enemy, firing off a few rounds to give Sam cover long enough to drag himself out of range.

Holding the plane in position, the pilot jumped out and ran to where Sam had taken cover. Sam continued firing round after round at the quickly approaching Nazi troops. When Sam turned to look at this remarkably brave and talented pilot, time stopped. He could have sworn it was George White. He blinked the sweat out of his eyes, certain it must be an illusion.

As his vision cleared, he could see that it wasn't George. This man was Lieutenant Dexter J. Jefferson, a member of the first Negro tactical-fighter squadron, the Tuskeegee Airmen. Sam noticed a calm but urgent expression on the man's face. The pilot moved with purpose, and hoisted Sam up on his shoulders. He quickly carried him to the aircraft, and slid him into the jump seat. As Sam crumpled into the seat, he noticed an old looking medallion with middle eastern, perhaps Egyptian script on the front had fallen from the pilot's neck and was hanging from the canopy window slot. Sam sensing an opportunity to return a good deed to this brave man quickly grabbed the medallion before it could fall to the ground and shoved it in his pocket. He would be sure and give it back to Lt. Jefferson when they returned to safety. Not noticing any of this Jefferson closed the canopy and secured himself in his seat prepared for a harrowing departure.

The Nazis were now only 150 yards away, and bullets whizzed by and riddled the P-51. They were bearing down fast. Jefferson cranked the engine once, twice, then a third time. With the Germans closing in, both men feared this might be their final moment.

Just then, the engine roared. The troops were only 100 yards away as Jefferson opened the plane's guns on them, spraying .90 mm fire. It was enough to slow the enemy's pursuit and bought them a few precious seconds. Brakes set, 20-degree flaps, and full power. The aircraft's engine bellowed like the roaring of an arctic wind, its canons blasting the whole way. The P-51 raced along the ground building speed, hopefully enough to clear the trees at the forest opening.

The troops falling quickly behind the fleeing aircraft were firing desperately in an attempt to stop them. Lieutenant Jefferson had one focus—the row of trees directly in front of him. The P-51's gear slowly began to lift off the ground. Twenty-five, thirty-five, forty feet higher they climbed, but a seventy-foot, majestic oak tree lay directly ahead. He couldn't clear it with altitude, so the Lieutenant quickly turned into a sixty-degree, sharp bank to the right and pulled back the stick. The P-51 veered away, just clipping a branch off the tree. Machine gun fire continued spraying all around as they headed due east and began their climb to safety. The bullet-riddled P-51 climbed to cruise altitude and leveled off on course for friendly airspace and returned to base.

The next thing Sam knew he was being awakened in a hospital bed with a throbbing pain from the deep gash in his thigh. His head was aching, and he was groggy as the sedatives and painkillers he'd been given wore off. He was disoriented as he looked around the room. There were injured soldiers everywhere, several worse off than he was. Many had lost entire limbs, had bandaged eyes, or appeared to be without any mental faculties.

He questioned what it was about war he had found noble. Was his own personal need for a vehicle for revenge worth this? Is that what all war stemmed from? He wondered if he could bring himself to return to the battlefield and to face more of the terror he had experienced. He had flashbacks of his buddies being slaughtered in the forest and trembled with horror, unable to rid himself of the bloody images racing through his mind. Then he thought about his rescue and how absolutely remarkable it was. When it was happening, he didn't have time to think about what was going on. In retrospect, it seemed a miracle that the fighter pilot was able to put his plane down in the middle of a battlefield and pull Sam from otherwise certain death. Equally as unexpected, that pilot was a Negro. A Negro, Sam shook his head, still trying to comprehend it.

In reviewing the events in his mind, Sam suddenly remembered the medallion that had fallen from the pilot's neck, and he panicked. He had to find the brave man who had saved his life. He wanted to thank him and return the unusual piece.

Sam called for the nurse. When she arrived he asked her the whereabouts of the pilot who had brought him there. She didn't have a clue who Sam was talking about or where he might be. When he finished describing the pilot to the best of his recollection, the nurse plainly stated she would find out what she could and report back with any information. In the meantime, she insisted he lay down and get some rest.

The next morning, Sam was awakened by the clattering of a breakfast cart being rolled up next to his bed by a hospital attendant. The nurse he had spoken to the day before was also making rounds. As she checked his vital signs, she mentioned that the only thing she was able to find out about the man who brought him in was that he was one of the "nigger" pilots. She then exclaimed incredulously, "I never knew they let niggers fly. How 'bout that."

Sam's heart dropped as he listened to the disrespectful way the nurse was talking about the most amazing man he had ever encountered. However, he had learned a long time ago to just swallow his anger and not say a word.

A few days later Sam was decorated with the Purple Heart and given an honorable discharge. Before he could leave, he had to find Jefferson and return the medallion that had snapped off of his neck. The medallion was mystical looking, almost alive. It really was a fascinating piece of work. The front was carved with the head of an eagle and in the center was an emerald that glowed as the light reflected off it.

After asking around, Sam located the pilot's barracks and immediately went there to find Lieutenant Jefferson. As he entered the barracks, there was only one man sitting on his cot. The colored soldier slowly looked up at Sam. "Can I help you?"

"Yes. I'm looking for someone—er, Lieutenant Jefferson. Do you know where I can find him?"

"Why are you looking for Jefferson?" the soldier asked, staring blankly at the floor.

"Well, Lieutenant Jefferson saved my life and in the process he lost this medallion. I just wanted to return it to him and thank him for pulling me out of that field."

"Well, I guess your luck is better than Dex's," the soldier curtly snapped back. "He was shot down and killed over Germany this morning."

Sam felt sick to his stomach. Somehow he felt responsible.

The soldier looked up at him. "I'm sorry. It's just that when Dexter was killed I lost a great friend."

Sam tried to hand the man the medallion but the soldier vehemently refused. He said the medallion was hexed, explaining that Dex had told everyone it had the power to protect whomever had possession of it. If that person lost it, he would perish. The soldier looked down at the medallion Sam was now holding with apprehension.

"I think it's probably best if you just hold onto that medallion—forever. I think you should be going now, soldier."

Sam just nodded, indicating he understood. He turned and walked away not knowing when, how, or if this mysterious, new treasure would ever impact his life. He made a vow to himself to never lose this jewel or forget how he obtained it. It would serve as a constant reminder of the bravery of Lieutenant Dexter Jefferson, the man who had saved his life.

3.

Sam was startled out of his daydream by a crashing noise off in the distance. He raised his head, questioning his hearing. He stood and walked over to the window to see if he could identify anything in the field behind the house.

With the storm pouring down outside, there wasn't much to see except the moisture from the rain glazing his dirty windows. He went to the front door and tried to get a better view. A loud crash of thunder shocked him. He continued out onto the covered porch, which sheltered the tiny cabin. As he struggled to see through the downpour, he began to question why he had come outside. Surely the crash he heard was no more than just the—

Sam shuddered as a lightning bolt flashed across the sky. The only sounds to be heard tonight were those of this dreadful storm, he thought.

As he turned to go into the house, he noticed a red flashing light off in the distance, then another light throbbing just beneath the flashing red one. The white light was blinking about twice the speed of the red. At first it appeared to be a sheriff's car, but the way the lights were flashing was more like an aircraft.

Sam's heart dropped into his stomach. An aircraft. He began running as fast as he could toward the flashing lights. His old, battle-worn legs stumbled and failed him every few steps as he approached the downed craft. He was driven by something he couldn't explain. The pouring rain drenching his tattered clothes, the savage thunder and lustrous bolts of lightning blurred into an imperceptible background as he grew closer to the plane. Sam was still a few hundred yards away from the blinking lights of the aircraft when he stopped to take a breath and gather himself. His focus had become razor sharp. He didn't notice anything but the rhythm of the throbbing lights and his distance from them.

Sam's worn down body, no longer able to run towards his fixation, slowed to a brisk walk. His mind flooded with questions. Where in the hell did this plane come from? Why is it here? Was it trying to land in my field? Sam recalled the time when the P-51 Mustang had come to his rescue in the European battlefield during World War II. The thought shot a dose of adrenaline through him, and again he began to run. He had not been this emotionally charged by an event in forty years, and he didn't really notice his exhaustion. He just did what his heart compelled him to do.

He could now make out the silhouette of the small aircraft, and it didn't seem to be severely damaged. The lights still flashing, he wondered if the pilot were alive. He also noticed the plane was resting with its front side against a tree. As he closed in, he could see there was, in fact, very little damage. There was also no indication the pilot had gotten out of the plane.

As he ran up to the airplane, he noticed the engine wasn't running and there was some minor damage to the front side. He quickly walked around to the left side to check the cockpit. As he looked in, he saw the pilot slumped back against the window. Sam ran back around to the cabin doors on the right side of the plane and frantically attempted to get them open.

He pulled and pounded for a few minutes without success. Looking around, he noticed one of the aircraft's propeller blades had dislodged. With some tugging and bending, he was finally able to break the blade free from its spinner. Returning to the cabin door, he pushed the blade into the door slot. With all his might he pulled the blade back to create leverage. The blade slipped out of the slot, and he stumbled back. Undeterred, he tried again. He pulled and pulled until he began to hear the door creaking open.

Sam flew backwards about eight feet and fell to the ground as the cabin door flung open. He immediately jumped up and leapt into the airplane's cabin. As he looked around inside, he noticed there were no passengers. He then moved toward the cockpit. His mind slowed down—every action so deliberate he seemed to be moving in slow motion. As he got close enough to see the pilot's face, Sam gasped and held his chest. The man's face was covered with blood from a large gash on his forehead. But the profuse bleeding was not what struck Sam. Looking into the pilot's face, he flashed back to the first time he saw Lieutenant Jefferson. Sam, almost in shock, took a second look at the pilot. Even through the blood, the pilot's dark skin was apparent.

Sam nudged the man with no response. He nudged him harder, wondering if he were still alive. The pilot let out a gasp. Actually, more like a deep, painful moan. As the pilot began to grumble, Sam sighed in relief.

In some strange way it seemed as though Sam's whole life had been leading up to this very moment. It felt like a chance for atonement, a squaring up with the universe for the second chance he'd been given that day on the battlefield.

Sam checked under the pilot's shirt to see if there were more open wounds. Fortunately, there weren't. Sam wedged his shoulder under the pilot's right arm so he could get enough leverage to lift him out of his seat. Barely conscious, the pilot began to babble incoherently. Sensing that the man would be okay, Sam smiled as he carried him from the plane.

Outside the aircraft, Sam propped the weary pilot up against the right wing. Lightly, he began shaking the pilot's head to try to get him fully conscious. For a moment, the pilot came to.

"Are you okay?" Sam asked.

"Yeah, I think I'm okay, but I can't move my arm."

"Who are ya and where ya headed?"

The pilot, still groggy, paused for a moment, as if he were trying to remember. "Adam...Adam Freeman," he replied Adam then looked up, quizzically gazing at him "Where am I? How did you find me?" The shock and exhaustion then caught up with Adam and he collapsed into Sam's arms.

Sam acted quickly to get Adam the medical attention he obviously needed. He again lifted him to his feet. Sam had forgotten about the torrential rain until now. In the few moments they had been out of the airplane, Adam too was soaked. Only half-conscious, Adam tried to move his feet to keep pace with Sam's walking, but relied mostly on the strength of Sam's back and legs to move him along.

The flat stretch of land they had to cross was littered with potholes and covered with tall, wild grasses. With the rain still pouring down heavily, maneuvering was difficult. Sam's heart burned with the desire to see this young man to safety before he could stop and rest. As they moved closer to the road at the edge of the field, Sam noticed headlights coming in their direction. He and Adam were still in the shadow of the tall grasses, and Sam knew chances were slim the car would actually see them. As the car sped by, Sam let out a sigh of fatigue. As determined as he was, he was still an old man, and the adrenaline that had driven him initially was beginning to fade.

Sam stopped for a moment to rest and tried to lay Adam down, but momentarily lost his grip. Adam hit the ground hard and groaned in pain.

"Oh my God!" Sam cried.

Sam fell to his knees to examine Adam. Although he was pretty banged up, he was still hanging on to consciousness. Once again, Sam gently hoisted Adam up on his shoulders and slowly began moving towards the road. Now only a couple hundred feet from the roadside, Sam began to feel energized. They were almost there. Now he could only hope someone would come along and pick them up, but on this road at this time of night, chances were pretty slim. Their last shot may have been the headlights that sped by a few minutes earlier.

Reaching the barbed-wire fence that enclosed the field, Sam contemplated how to get Adam over without scratching him all to hell. After a moment of pondering, Sam removed his flannel shirt and his undershirt. He folded them in half and then in half again. Laying the folded shirts on top of the fence, Sam lifted Adam up and laid him across the shirts to protect him from the barbed wire. He then whispered into Adam's ear, "Hold on, this might hurt a little bit."

He gave Adam a shove that slid him over onto the other side. When Adam hit the ground he let out a loud grunt and began grumbling and groaning. Sam smiled, knowing the hard part was over. If Adam were still alive at this point, there was a good chance he would make it the rest of the way.

He reached through the fence and grabbed the shirts now laying on the ground on the other side. He put them back on top of the fence and leaned on top of them. Just as he had done with Adam, he slid himself over the fence to the other side. He, too, hit the ground rather hard, but no damage was done. He walked over to the road and looked in both directions to see if any vehicles were approaching. No such luck. He waited a bit longer, and still nothing. He figured he'd better keep moving to get Adam to safety. Although the rain had let up a bit, it was still coming down pretty hard.

As Sam lifted Adam again, he noticed how much more difficult it was. He was growing weary. Now, all he had was the drive that burned deep in his heart. He had to get this man to safety if it was the last thing he did. He had to do it.

Adam's feet again began moving as he slipped in and out of consciousness. Sam comforted him with his gentle words.

"I'll get you there, son. You just hold tight. I'll die before I'll leave you out here. It means too much to both of us."

Sam began focusing on the road ahead. Off in the distance he could see a faint light. He stopped for a moment to bring it into clear view. The light wasn't moving, so he figured it wasn't a car. Looking harder, it appeared to be a house. The adrenaline began pumping and he started panting as he picked up the pace toward the light in the distance. Sam felt as though God himself were carrying the two of them now. It wouldn't be long—just a little bit farther.

4.

"Marlena, could you please grab the butter out of the fridge?" the voice rang out from the dining room.

"Okay. You guys need anything else?"

"No, honey, I think that's it. Thanks."

Marlena walked into the dining room as her mother, Sara, an attractive, middle-aged woman, was serving pasta to her disgruntled husband.

"I can't believe this town. The place is filled with bigots," he said, rubbing the thining hair on top of his head. As he sat in his seat Austin, shifted his tall frame slightly away from the table and unbuttoned his slightly tight trousers to accommodate his meal.

"Austin Thompson, I guess you prefer a more subtle brand of bigot, like your cohorts back east."

"Mom, what are you guys talking about?" Marlena interrupted.

"Well, dear, your father is rattled about the editorial that was printed in his newspaper today." She finished with a compassionate glance toward Austin, adjusting her short brown hair behind her ear. Her hazel eyes gave him a warm, safe haven to focus while he continued to vent.

"It's the people in this damn town, Marlena. They're just so ignorant. An editorial was printed today that shouldn't have been. The thing that burns me up the most about it is that it was kept from me in the prepress meeting. Hank knew if he showed me the piece I would have rejected it," Austin said.

"Oh yeah. I read that and wondered how it got printed. I thought maybe you took the week off or something," Marlena said with a bit of sarcasm. "Well, Dad, look at it this way, at least now your paper is reflecting the majority views of the community."

"I should just fire Hank and be done with it. Of course, it would take six months to get someone to replace him."

"So go ahead and make a statement, Austin. Fire him! We'll help out at the newspaper any way we can," Sara chimed in.

"No, I can't. As backwards as his ideology is, he is an awfully good assistant editor, and it would be too much of a financial burden on his family. Let's just drop it. I'll have a talk with him tomorrow."

"Dad, how are you ever going to make a difference in this town if you continue to let things like this slide? At some point you have to make a stand. I guess you've forgotten some of the things you taught me."

"Marlena, I said let's drop it. I don't want to go into this any further. I would like to sit here and enjoy the wonderful meal you've prepared, thank you."

"Yes, Marlena, this pasta primavera is absolutely wonderful."

"Thanks for the compliment, you guys, but dad, I think you're dodging the subject."

"You're welcome. I thought maybe you missed it in your moment of high morality. Well, enough about my problems. How is Eve's favorite grade school teacher doing?" Austin asked.

"Everything is going pretty well. There is, however, one student I wish I could spend more time with. He is absolutely brilliant in class but he rarely turns in his home work assignments and he misses a lot of classes."

"Have you tried contacting his parents?"

"I don't need to. Every time I keep him after normal school hours, his mother shows up. I can never talk to her because she is always so curt. It's like she thinks I'm trying to steal him from her or something."

"Well, why don't you give him some guidance? She probably feels threatened, " Sara said, "Most of the blacks in this town don't feel like they have any future. They are in dead-end jobs. Their parents don't have the wherewithal to further their own educations beyond the basics they get in these small, underfunded schools. For God's sake, it was only three years ago the state stepped in and made this town integrate the school system. There has been generation after generation of people with no hope of doing anything more than surviving from day to day. The ones that do get a chance to succeed usually pack up their families and escape from this hellhole as quickly as they can, which leaves no mentorship at all. So the cycle continues."

His interest now raised, Austin said, "So, Sara, you're the social scientist. What can we do to stimulate progress in this town?"

She shrugged"I've thought about it a great deal and I have some ideas, but I haven't worked out how to effectively initiate them."   "I think I have pretty much resolved to building the newspaper as much as I can and selling it, so we can get back on our feet and return to the East Coast," Austin said.

"Austin, I can't believe what I'm hearing," Sara said. "I don't care if we only plan on being here one more day. We can't just stand by and accept the status quo. In case you've forgotten, a long time ago we vowed to make a difference on this planet. I didn't think that meant selective segments we can pick and choose as the cause fits our convenience. I will no longer sit and watch as this godforsaken place keeps itself in the nineteenth century."

"Sara, what about all the Klan activity? What do we do with those people?"

"Is that what you're afraid of?"

"Those people are terrorists," Austin replied, shaking his head. "There is no telling what they would do to you and Marlena if I pushed too hard. I just don't want to jeopardize my family."

"What are you really afraid of?" Sara replied. "Remember the editorial you did on organized crime at the *Times*? You weren't afraid for our lives then, or you felt confident we could handle it. What has changed?"

"I don't know. I just don't know." Austin bowed his head, looking at his plate of pasta in despair.

Sara walked over and hugged him around the shoulders. "I'm sorry, but some of the practices of this town are absolutely unacceptable. I can't stay here any longer not doing anything. Anyway, whether we plan to stay here or not, we are here now. I am beginning to feel a need do whatever I can while I'm here to help this town be more civilized."

"What are you going to do, Mom?" Marlena said.

"Well, for now let's just leave it at I'm going to do something. Don't be surprised if I ask for your help."

"Sure, I'd love to. It will be like when I was a kid and you took me to the city on your social work visits."

Sara nodded. "Yes, honey, I did enjoy your company while I was on those trips. Even then you were very helpful."

"She's always gotten along with just about everyone. Unless of course you are talking about a husband," Austin added with a smile.

"Be careful, Dad. You never know who your son-in-law will be if you marry me off in this town."

"Oh, I don't know," Austin responded. "That Brad fellow isn't such a bad guy."

"Lord knows, the entire town wants you two together," Sara added.

"I am not interested in marrying Brad," Marlena said.

"Is there anyone you are interested in marrying, Marlena?" Sara said, raising an eyebrow. "You know, you aren't getting any younger. Is that young man who travels so much still sending you letters? Oh, what's his name?" she said in frustration

"Yes, Mother, Brian still writes to me occasionally. We have always been really good friends."

Just as Sara began to respond, Marlena snapped, "Just friends, Mother," then added, "When the right man shows himself to me I'll know. So let's just give it a—"

At that instant they heard a loud thud on the porch.

"What was that?" Sara said, frightened.

Reassuringly, Marlena said, "It's probably just that old wooden statue," Marlena replied. "It's always getting knocked over by the wind, and it seems like there is quite a storm out there. I'll get it."

"My goodness," Sara said, glancing out of the dining room window. "I hadn't noticed how hard it was raining outside."

As Marlena walked towards the entrance, someone began banging loudly on the door.

"I wonder who that could be?" Austin said.

As Marlena grew closer to the door, she could hear a gruff voice.

"Please, help us."

Marlena sprinted to the door and without thinking grabbed the door handle and vigorously swung it open. Sensing trouble, Austin and Sara quickly got up and rushed to the door. Marlena stood looking at two drenched men in tattered clothing. An old man, exhausted, looked up at the three of them and with what little energy he could muster said, "This man needs help."

Both the old man and a younger man then collapsed in the doorway.

5.

"Sara, call an ambulance," Austin shouted, and knelt down next to the two men around whom a large pool of blood, water, and mud had formed.

"Sir, are you okay?" He asked as he lightly shook the old man's head and waited for a response.

Breathing heavily, the old man opened his eyes and answered, "I'm just exhausted. I'll be fine, but this man's been in a plane crash. Make sure he gets to a doctor."

Marlena knelt next to her father to tend to the bleeding gash on the young man's temple. Sara had gone to the other room to call for help and returned frantically screaming, "The darn 911 number is out of order and there is no answer at the sheriff's office."

Austin remained calm "We'll just have to take them ourselves. Sara, go bring the car around to the front. Be sure to pull it as close to the porch as you can."

"Okay!" she answered and hurried out through the back door.

"Marlena, let me see if he is conscious," Austin said as he motioned her to move aside. He then tilted the young man's head back. "Well, he's breathing. That's a good sign."

Looking down at his face, Austin said, "Plane crash, huh? I assume it must have been a light aircraft and this man was the only passenger on board.

"Or the pilot," Marlena said.

"Yeah, that's what I meant. I've just never met a black pilot before," he pondered aloud, "and certainly would have preferred to do so under other circumstances. Are you conscious?" Austin asked, gently moving the young man's head back and forth. Again he shook him. "Sir, can you hear me?" His voice was a little louder the second time, and the man began to stir.

He slowly lifted his head as he began to grumble, "Where the hell am I? How did I get here?"

"Your plane crashed and you're in our home," Austin said. "What's your name, son?"

"Adam, Adam Freeman." It seemed to take all of his strength just to answer.

Marlena began to smile. Almost in a trance, she sat silently watching as Austin continued.

"How do you feel, Adam?"

"I feel okay. I should try to get back to my aircraft now." His half-raised body collapsed back into Austin's arms.

Sara scurried back into the house and breathlessly announced,

"The car is ready, Austin. What do you need us to do?"

Austin turned toward Sara. "Can you and Marlena handle helping the old man to the car? I'll bring Adam."

As Austin lifted Adam and carried him to the car, the two women went over to the older man. Sara nudged him a couple of times and he began to stir.

"Can you move?" Sara asked.

"I'm exhausted, not crippled." He said gruffly.

They helped him to his feet and he leaned on their shoulders as they went out to the car.

6.

A medical attendant entered the room, and her voice gently sang in a sweet, southern drawl, "Mr. Freeman, would you care for some breakfast? We brought you just about everything we could think of. There's eggs, bacon, toast, danish, pastries, juice, and coffee. We didn't know what you'd like, so we tried to cover all of the basics. I hope you find something here that will suit your fancy," she finished with a hint of flirtation.

Adam, still a bit hazy and in quite a bit of pain, simply smiled and nodded. The attendant, a rather plain-looking black woman in her twenties, flashed back a smile and walked out of the room.

Moments later another woman came in. This one was dressed in pink nurse's attire holding a clipboard. "How is our pilot doing this morning?"

Again, Adam could only muster a nod in response, indicating he was doing pretty well.

"Well, you're not too bad off," she responded. "You've got a pretty bad concussion and you fractured a couple ribs. You also sustained a few lacerations and bruises, all of them minor. You'll be a little sore for awhile, but you'll be all right. I brought you something for pain."

She handed him some pills in a small paper cup. He took the cup and popped the pills into his mouth. He washed them down with the glass of juice on his breakfast tray. He looked back up at the nurse. "How long are you planning to keep me here?"

The nurse replied, "That's up to the doctor. He'll be in to see you a little later."

Adam looked at the telephone sitting on the nightstand. He sat there quietly, wondering who he should call first. He wasn't looking forward to telling anyone he had just crashed his prized Malibu Mirage. His mom would be terrified. He toyed with the idea of not telling her what happened and simply feigning perfect health. She had been leery of him flying ever since his first lesson. He decided the best person to call would be his girlfriend, Donna. He picked up the phone and dialed, then sat silently as it rang.

"Come on, girl, pick up the damn phone," he said quietly.

Just then he heard a voice on the other end. "Hello?" The voice was a lot deeper than Adam was expecting.

"Who is this?" Adam asked in a perturbed tone.

Suddenly, he heard a woman's voice snap on the other end, "Give me that, I didn't say you could answer my phone. Hello?"

"Donna, who in the hell was that that answered the phone?"

"That was just Tyrone. Don't worry baby, he's just a friend of mine," she replied.

"A friend. It's seven o'clock in the goddamn morning, girl. What kind of friend comes over this early? He sounded like he just woke up. What kind of fool do you take me for? What's going on over there?"

Donna responded in the sweetest tone she could muster,

"Adam, don't be jealous, nothing happened. Tyrone was over and it got late so he just slept on the couch. It's nothing, baby."

Adam could hear the man giggling in the background. Furious, Adam held the receiver away from his ear, looking at it with disdain. If he could have smashed it into a thousand little bits, he would have. He put the phone back to his ear. Donna, on the other end, was still trying to smooth things over.

"Adam, I love you, baby. I told you after the last time that I wouldn't let anything like that happen again. Tyrone is just a friend. Please, please," she begged in a sappy tone, "don't be mad."

He heard the man's voice in the background say, "Yeah, Adam, don't be mad, there's plenty for everybody. You don't want to let this fine honey go Ha, ha."

Adam could not say a word. He could only feel the pain swelling inside himself. He managed to lift the receiver he had let slip into his lap and said, "Donna, I gotta go. I'll talk to you later. He quickly hung up.

Adam stared up at the ceiling. What a day. What next? He sat there on the clinic bed, silently pondering his next move. As the morning went on, not only did his heart hurt but the pain from his injuries was becoming more noticeable. He decided he had to call Martin Swift, the man he was to meet in Friday Harbor the following morning. He needed to tell him he was going to be delayed. Then it occurred to him. How long was he going to be here? For that matter, where was here?

He looked up toward the doorway and in walked an older black gentleman wearing a brown suit. The man was tall and clean shaven. He walked with self-assurance and purpose. Adam noticed the man was carrying a Bible.

"Good morning, young brother," the man cheerfully greeted Adam.

"Good morning, sir," Adam replied.

"I hear you had quite a night last night, son." He said as he removed the brown derby that hid his salt and pepper colored hair. "I can't say I've ever met anyone who has survived a plane crash. 'Course it looks suspiciously to me like somebody," he gestured toward the ceiling, "wants you to be around here for a while. I think it was destiny for a man with your name to crash in this town," the man said with a devilish grin.

Adam looked at the stranger, a bit confused. "What do you mean, a man with my name?"

The man smiled. "Adam, allow me to welcome you to Eve. Eve, Louisiana."

"Get out of here. Are you serious? That's kind of wild." Adam thought for a moment, then continued, "Well, sir, I hate to disappoint you, but I won't be here for long. So, I doubt that destiny will get much chance to have its way with me. By the way, you know who I am, but who are you?"

"My name is Reverend Jes Jacobson. I am the pastor of the First Baptist Church here in Eve. Quite honestly, son, I believe that you were sent here for a purpose. Our people could use a man with your skills and knowledge here. Eve is a nice, quiet town as long as you don't make any trouble. We need a man like you to teach the younger generation they have a chance—that they can be more than a day laborer in the fields, or a handyman, or gardener. Not that there is anything wrong with those jobs. They are honest, decent jobs, but there is so much more."

He leaned in a bit closer and continued. "For the most part, the blacks here feel like they have the best jobs they can ever get. As long as they believe that, they're right. Now you can show these youngsters firsthand what they can do if they focus their energy and aim high. The best way to break the chains around the souls of the youth in this town is for them to have hope, and Adam, that hope fell out of the sky last night and landed in a field just north of town." The reverend nodded at Adam.

Adam sat silently for a moment, totally taken aback. Just eighteen hours ago he was flying to the Pacific Northwest to live out his dream. Two hours ago he was awakened by a stranger serving him breakfast in a medical facility. Now this—appointed black messiah in a town that, up until an hour ago, he never knew existed.

After a few more moments Adam responded, "Reverend, with all due respect, I already have a life. I am on my way to the San Juan Islands in northern Washington. I have an appointment with a gentleman who is interested in backing the purchase of a small airport. That is what I feel my life has been leading me to for the last fifteen years. I really would love to help out in any way I can, but you must realize my stay here is temporary and there is only so much a man can do for a cause in one or two days."

"Son, from what I understand of your circumstances, you're gonna be here longer than you think. Your plane is pretty badly banged up. The authorities are on their way to do an investigation, and from the looks of you right now, you won't be ready to travel for awhile." He smiled. "I understand, Adam, that this must be a big shock for you. I must seem like I'm coming on a bit strong, but all I'm asking is for you to share a little of yourself with us while you're here, nothing more. I don't really expect a lifelong commitment or anything. Just give it some thought, all right, son?"

Adam, realizing the magnitude of his circumstances, simply nodded.

Before leaving, the reverend said, "Adam, may God bless you and everyone you meet. Our church service is at 9 a.m. on Sunday. It would be my honor if you could make it. You take care of yourself."

Again, all Adam could muster was a dazed nod. He lay there on the bed after Reverend Jacobson left, solemnly pondering his situation. There was no time for despair as his thoughts shifted to all the things he would have to do to get his plans back on track.

The first matter of business was all of the calls he still had to make. He needed to call his financial backer, Dennis Knockle, who was meeting him tomorrow at the Seattle airport. Then there was the airport director, Martin Swift, the man who was to give him the tour of the facilities. Maybe he could convince Tony, his airplane mechanic, to come down and work on the Piper—'43 Alpha Lima. He didn't even know how badly his aircraft had been damaged, if at all.

Suddenly he began to feel overwhelmed by everything he had to do. He knew he needed to get on top of the situation right away. He picked up the phone and dialed.

"Hello?"

"Hey, Mom, what's goin on?"

"Adam, is that you? You sound like you're sick, baby. Are you all right?"

Adam hesitated. He didn't want to startle his mother, so he chose his words carefully. "I was in a little accident, Mom. Everything is okay. Nobody was hurt."

"You were in a car accident? Where are you? I thought that you were on your way to Washington. Who was driving?"

What Adam had intended as just a friendly call quickly turned to hysterics. "Mom, I am on my way to Washington. I had to put my Malibu down in a field during a storm. I'm in a clinic, but just for a few tests. Please don't worry, Ma, I am perfectly fine."

Adam's mother was fighting to keep her wits about her so she wouldn't become completely hysterical. "Adam, you were in a plane crash?"

Adam could hear his dad in the background exclaim, "Plane crash? Who was in a plane crash?"

The situation was snowballing to the point that it was almost comical. "Mom, let's just call it a forced landing. I am not hurt. My aircraft is fine. I'll be out of here in a couple of days."

Not believing a word, she retorted, "If you're so fine, why are they keeping you in the hospital for two days? Adam, where are you? Your father and I will fly right down there to see you."

Adam was touched by his mother's concern, and it brought a smile to his face. "Mom, seriously, the NTSB may be down here for a brief investigation, and that's why I've got to stick around. The Piper may need a week, but other than that, everything is in order. I really appreciate your concern, Ma, but everything is under control."

Relieved, she said, "Adam, you know from the very moment you first decided to fly I've been a nervous wreck. I know it's just my own fear and that flying an airplane is statistically safer than driving a car. I just care for you, baby, and if anything ever happened to you, I would die. Anyway, I'm supposed to go first. You know I would trade my life in a moment so you could have a full, rich, and very long life. Please, please, please, please, promise me you'll be careful."

Touched, Adam willingly obliged. "Okay, Mom, I'll be careful. Listen, I just woke up and I don't even know the exact name of the hospital I'm in. The name of the town is Eve. I'll call you later on with the phone number where I'll be. Okay?"

There was silence and then she replied, "Eve, where is that?"

"Louisiana. Everything happened so fast I will have to look at my charts to tell you exactly where it is. But hey, Mom, I've got a lot of important calls to make, so I'll call you sometime this evening. I know Dad wants to talk. Just tell him I'll talk to him tonight when I call. I love you. Tell Dad the same for me, would you?"

"Okay, baby, I'll tell him. I love you, too!"

"Bye, Ma."

"Bye-bye, Adam."

After the call to his mother, Adam had the energy he needed to make his remaining business calls. He was able to get all of his meetings at the airport in Friday Harbor moved back a week. Everyone was understanding and sympathetic about his situation. His long-time friend and airplane mechanic wasn't able to fly down and take a look at the Malibu. Instead, he would send someone else who was just as capable.

Adam could see some resolution to his current predicament. Now the question was how long all of this was going to take, and when could he get out of this town?

Just as Adam began to contemplate his next move, a stone came smashing through his window. He heard laughter coming from below his room outside. Not having his full strength, he could do no more than sit up in shock, staring at the shattered pane.

In rushed the attendant and the nurse.

"Oh my God, Mr. Freeman, are you all right?" the nurse exclaimed with a deep, southern drawl.

Adam was becoming accustomed to the southern accent prevalent in this area. Everyone he had talked to so far had it. "Yeah, yeah, I'm fine. I'm just a little shaken up, that's all," he responded.

The attendant walked over to pick up the stone that had come through the window and noticed it had a piece of paper around it, wrapped with twine. The nurse and the attendant were joined by Doctor Hankin, who had just walked in the room, as they studied the message. The attendant handed the doctor the note. He read it silently. When he was finished, he could only shake his head in disgust. He walked over to Adam and asked the nurse and the attendant to excuse themselves, which they promptly did.

"Mr. Freeman, I realize these are not particularly good circumstances for you." The doctor hesitated. "Where you're from, you probably have the respect of your neighbors and other people who look up to you for what you've accomplished. You seem pretty bright, and being a pilot, it's obvious you have achieved some things in your life. Frankly, Adam, this town has a real problem with race relations. It's not something I'm particularly proud of, but it seems I'm in the minority on the subject. I'm here because my family is here and my folks don't have much time left. Well, I don't want to get wrapped up in my story. What I'm getting at, Adam, is there are more bigots and racists in this town than perhaps anywhere in the country. If I were you, I would find a way to leave this town as quickly as I could."

Adam was momentarily in shock, but then exploded. "You mean to tell me not only am I laid up in this place with broken ribs, but I'm in a town I've never heard of, I have no idea what shape my aircraft is in, I'm going to be a week late to the biggest meeting of my life, and I have drifted into a twilight zone where a lynch mob is going to drag me out of bed and string me up in the town square? Is that what your telling me, Doc?"

The doctor flashed Adam a grin to comfort him."Well, if it's any relief, I looked over your X-rays and there is no sign of breakage. So, there is some good news. Also, from what I hear, your airplane was pretty much intact when they pulled you out. As far as the lynching goes, we haven't experienced anything that severe here in many years."

"Oh, but you have experienced them? Now I'm relieved, Doc. That really did the trick," Adam snapped back.

"Adam, I'm sorry if I've startled you with this information. It's not like we have nightly cross burnings in the center of town. However, there are a number of citizens in this community still acting like this is the 1850s. Those people will be incredibly threatened by a Negro, er, um, African-American of your caliber and professional aptitude. They will make every moment of your stay here as unpleasant as possible."

Adam looked up at the doctor. "What does the note say, Doc?"

Dr. Hankin reached down and handed Adam the note. Before Adam had a chance to read any of it, Dr. Hankin said, "Adam, this is by no means reflective of the overall feelings in this town towards black people. There are a lot of wonderful people here. You just need to be careful about who you choose to fraternize with. We will probably release you from the clinic sometime tomorrow. You should be well enough to get along by then. If you aren't able to leave Eve right away, and have any trouble finding lodging, just call me here at the clinic. I might be able to help. It was very nice to meet you, Adam. Best of luck."

"Thank you," Adam replied, and looked up at the ceiling as if to ask for some divine guidance. Glancing back to the cryptic note Dr. Hankin had handed him, he began to read:

Dear Nigger, you fell out of the sky once already. The next time we're gonna help you and there'll be a rope around your neck when we do. Get out of town or else!

7.

Adam lay in his bed at the clinic pondering the past twenty-four hours. He couldn't put any reason to the events that led up to his current condition or circumstances. He kept wondering what he'd done wrong to deserve this. This was supposed to be the best time of his life, and for all he knew it could be shot. He had nightmares about the Klan riding up and dragging him out of his bed to be lynched. He wondered if his life were meant to end in this small, southern enclave of bigotry. His feelings vacillated between utter terror and rage.

He never envisioned himself being so vulnerable to racial censure, especially when it could lead to his ultimate death. How in the world had he ended up here? Why now? He looked up and stared out the window, trying to see around the plastic that replaced the broken glass. For the moment all seemed hopeless.

"Good afternoon, Mr. Freeman," echoed a cheerful voice.

Adam, taken by surprise, glanced around. When he saw he had a visitor, he was at a loss for words and could only manage a meager, "Hi."

The man approached Adam, reaching over to shake his hand. "Do you mind if I call you Adam?"

"No, not at all," he said as he shook the man's hand. Adam wondered who the hell he was?

"Adam, my name is Austin Thompson."

Austin turned and faced the two women following him into the room. He gestured toward them. "This is my wife, Sara, and my daughter, Marlena."

As Austin continued to speak, gesturing dramatically with his long arms, Adam looked over at the two women. They, too, were quite cheerful. They had flowers and a basket of food they were placing on the table opposite his bed. He was immediately taken by both of their beauty and awakened by the vivid color of their sun-dresses and the suppleness within them. Both had smooth light olive complexions. Their similarity to one another as striking as their loveliness. Both moved gracefully through the room with strides filled with vibrance. Even the older seemed as if she could hike Mt. Rainier at an instant.

As Adam lay, taking in their loveliness, he felt a surge of energy shoot through his body. His gaze caught the younger Ms. Thompson as she leaned over to adjust the basket so it wouldn't tip over. She tilted her head and caught Adam's gaze. Their eyes met and locked. Adam was stunned by the depth of the feeling he had as he looked into Marlena's twinkling eyes. Mr. Thompson was rambling on, but at this moment, it was nothing more than background noise. She flashed Adam a friendly smile. Adam was so taken by Marlena's beauty he just sank back into his fluffed pillow and tried to regain his composure.

He attempted to refocus on Mr. Thompson's comments with little success.

"…and so, if you need, you are more than welcome to be our houseguest until your airplane is flight worthy. We really would love to have you."

Mrs. Thompson seconded the invitation. "Mr. Freeman, with the Blossom Festival taking place this week, you'll be hard-pressed to find a place to stay within 75 miles of Eve. Quite honestly, I don't believe you could find any place as hospitable as our home, so please consider it."

The warmth of Sara's smile put Adam at ease.

"Excuse me for being rude," Adam said, "but where did you people come from? I was just told I should get out of town before I get lynched, and in walks the friendliest family in America, rolling out the red carpet. I don't get it. Somebody missed telling me something."

The demurely beautiful Marlena Thompson tried to explain.

"Mr. Freeman, we brought you here last night—"

"Oh, so you're the one who dragged me from the plane? Thank you so much—"

"No, Mr. Freeman. A gentleman named Sam actually pulled you out of your airplane and carried you about three miles to our home. We just brought you to the clinic from there. As for your lynching, there are a few of us in this town who fervently stand against any form of bigotry. If anyone is planning on lynching anyone, they better plan on walking through the hellfire of Marlena Thompson to get there!"

Sara flashed Adam a wink, "And she's a pussycat compared to me!"

Turning to Adam, Austin smiled. "Well, I feel safe," he said. "How about you?"

Adam's earlier tensions were relieved, and he smiled and thanked the Thompsons for their offer, adding that he really didn't know how long he would be in town. If he was going to be there for any period of time after his release from the clinic, he said he would seriously consider the invitation.

Unable to take his eyes off Marlena, Adam had to take a deep breath to calm himself because of the way his heart was racing. Her brunette hair and big, beautiful green eyes had him so distracted he couldn't think. To make eye contact with Marlena was to fall into her soul. With every glance, he felt a little of himself changed. He became a little gentler in the presence of this woman, and perhaps for the first time he experienced being enveloped by God's tenderness and compassion. He noticed the fullness of her lips and how perfectly they matched her sculpted cheekbones. She had a smooth, light olive complexion. The effect she had on him was eerie.

Every time he looked at her he felt his insides tremble. He glanced over at her sleeveless dress—white with a bright floral print—and tried to refrain from shaking his head in appreciation. He noticed how her dress flowed gently over her well-defined curves as she moved. Her arms and legs were athletic and shapely. He tried not to stare, and no one seemed to notice his affliction.

The conversation turned to Adam's health. Adam explained he just had a couple of bruised ribs and that basically he felt fine. The mood was light and Adam's discomfort with his situation was all but gone now. Before leaving, Sara was able to charm Adam into committing to being their guest, at least for his first night out of the clinic. Upon finishing their good-byes, Sara added that she wanted to make a special dinner in Adam's honor the following evening.

After the Thompsons left his room, Adam just lay there in awe of how friendly these people had been toward him. Even in his extensive travels as a pilot, he was never able to let down his emotional guard long enough for there to be any intimacy with someone of another race. It was remarkable how Sara was able to immediately disarm him. They treated him as though he were a member of their family. His thoughts then shifted to Marlena. That woman is fine.

Adam had a hard time concentrating on anything. His mind kept going back to the smile she had flashed him when their eyes met. He thought about her incessantly but couldn't bring himself to believe anything could ever happen between them. He rationalized that he would not be in town long enough to get anything started and even if he could, this town would not tolerate a relationship between a white girl as beautiful as Marlena and him. The truth of the matter was that Adam was terrified of Marlena. Even with all he had accomplished in his career, at the core of his belief about himself was an oppressed, ghetto boy who could never really accept that he belonged alongside his white peers.

This view of himself had begun forming even before he could speak. These were his parents' views, and their parents' views, and on down the line. Not many days passed as a child when he didn't hear his mom, dad, or someone else say something like, "Don't trust whitey. That white man sure knows what he's doin'. The white man's still ahead. The white man's got all the power. What will the White man think of next? If I was white, I would have gotten that job. They just don't like us," and finally, "Even if you get a white girl to go out with you, the moment something goes wrong she'll be calling you nigger just like the rest of them."

These subconscious voices had been with him for years, and whenever he got too sure of himself, they would surface. Adam typically dated within his race, although in discussions with others he would always give lip service to being open to dating other races. The truth of the matter was, although open to it, he was very unsure of what he had to offer anyone with culture and refinement. He unconsciously feared he would be found out as the shallow, uncultured, ghetto boy he was, and the object of his desire would move on to someone more suitable. It really was a sad way to live, but it was Adam's only way of protecting himself, or so his ego thought.

By the time he finished thinking about his day, and the wonderful visit he had with the Thompsons, he had talked himself out of considering any involvement with Marlena. He would be a respectful and appreciative guest, get his aircraft repaired, and be on his way.

8.

"Are you sure this is the only vehicle you have available? A 1980 Chevy Citation? You gotta be kidding me. I barely remember that car. That's the ugly, slope-backed car, isn't it? What kind of rental car company is this?"

"Sir, that is the only car left for you to rent. Do you want it or not?" she responded curtly.

Adam mumbled to himself, "I have got to get out of this damn place. I know what's up. I have got to go." He then looked pensively back in the woman's direction. "I'll take the car."

He filled out the necessary paperwork and went on his way. The car was hard to start and, when it did, it had a terrible smell of fumes. Adam was accustomed to driving his Porsche Carrera and flying his own high-performance Piper Malibu aircraft, not to mention DC 10s, private Lear jets, and Cessna Citations. This vehicle was painfully slow to Adam, and he could hardly bear it.

He looked down at the directions scribbled on a notepad and followed them to the Thompsons' home. He was looking forward to seeing these people again, but his old views still haunted him. He couldn't totally relax and trust these seemingly lovely people, the only reason being that they were white. He ultimately felt they would turn on him in some way like so many others had.

He knocked on the door.

"Hello," responded a cheerful voice.

Adam stood there in silence, not knowing whether to be scared to death or completely joyous about seeing his new acquaintances.

The older of the Thompson beauties opened the front door. "Hello, Adam. Welcome to our humble home. You do look a lot better now."

"Well!" Adam shot back jokingly and smiled.

Sara returned the smile. "I meant no offense, Adam. You do, however, look ten times better today than you did a couple of evenings ago when Sam dragged you in from that awful storm."

"Yes, Mrs. Thompson, I know. No offense taken."

"Do you have any bags to be brought in?"

Adam shook his head. "No, this is everything." He held up two duffel bags. "I picked them up when I swung by the Malibu—my airplane—on my way here. I wanted to take a look at it to see how bad it is."

"Malibu?" Sara asked, a bit puzzled.

Tickled, he smiled. "My airplane is a Piper Malibu. It's like saying Ford Taurus or Chevy Impala. It's just the name of the aircraft."

"Oh, I see. It must be a pretty fancy..." she paused for a moment then continued, applying her newly-acquired jargon "aircraft, with a name like Malibu."

"Well, Mrs. Thompson, it is. It's the type of aircraft some people dream about. I know I did before I could actually afford to buy one."

"How is your aircraft?

"Oh, it's all right. It's seen better days, but after a forced landing in the conditions I was flying in, I feel fortunate that 43 Alpha is still intact. It seems like it's in better shape than I am. I still feel pretty banged up. I don't know the extent of the damage, but I don't anticipate it will take more than a couple of days to repair, once my mechanic gets here."

Sara showed Adam around their home. It was a beautiful house, to say the least. It had a large porch that wrapped around the white exterior. All of the rooms were decorated in a country motif, with floral prints in the washrooms. In the backyard was Mr. Thompson's hammock, strung between two giant oak trees. Just off the porch was a ten-foot white trellis with some sort of ivy growing to the top. There was also a bench swing facing a small pond in the middle of the yard. Adam was thinking about how lucky he was that every hotel in the area was booked. These were definitely deluxe accommodations.

It was still early in the afternoon, and Sara showed Adam to his room and suggested he might enjoy a nap until everyone returned home from work. He agreed and was grateful for some time alone to collect his thoughts and rest.

He lay across the guest bed in the room situated at the back of the house. Looking out the window, he saw the trees supporting Mr. Thompson's hammock. He noticed the leaves gently rustling in the wind. The sun was shining on them as they moved and they shimmered like so many oceans he had flown over in the past. He shifted his gaze to his room. He felt very comfortable here. His bed had four posts, reaching almost to the ceiling, and there was a shear fabric draped over the top. The plush dubonnet was white with a yellow check pattern and had violets with green stems. The bed was filled with pillows in all shapes and sizes. He looked at the dresser and the dainty trinkets on top. It was quite a guest room. He heard a gust of wind outside and his gaze shifted back to the shimmering leaves. He relaxed and his mind began to drift.

He thought of all of the things he had been through in the past two days and began to shudder. He felt fortunate just to be alive. Even though he felt pressure to finish what he had set out to do in Washington, the beauty of this moment struck him. He began thinking maybe he didn't have to try to force any outcomes. Maybe his fate was already planned. Maybe all he had to do was watch for the signs and follow them—just do what felt comfortable.

Indeed, the thought was quite appropriate, because the one thing Adam now felt was comfortable. He could smell the potpourri that sat on top the dresser. The aroma of gardenia and the warm summer breeze put Adam in a blissful trance. His thoughts floated to his last vision of the enchanting Marlena—the way she looked, the way she moved, and her heavenly smile. It made him all warm inside. He tried to push down his feelings, but to push them down meant only to build a powder keg inside himself. He thought of her and smiled. He drifted off into the most restful sleep he'd had in some time.

9.

Adam awoke to the smell of freshly baked bread. His forehead was beaded with sweat brought on by the heat and humidity. Looking out the window, he noticed the fiery-orange sun fading behind the trees to the west.

Still groggy from his afternoon siesta, Adam lay still for a moment, allowing himself to take in all the wonderful sensations. He didn't really understand why he felt such bliss. He thought about how friendly and genuine the Thompsons were toward him and could see no apparent reason for their helpfulness. He wondered what they could possibly have to gain. He decided to keep an open mind, but also to not get swept off of his feet until he was more certain about the Thompsons' motivations. However, he leaned toward the part of himself that felt secure that the Thompsons were indeed as genuine as they appeared.

He finally dragged himself out of bed and walked down a short hallway to the bathroom. The bathroom was fairly small. It had an old, oval pedestal tub and a white shower curtain with a delicate red, yellow, and green print. The floor was white tile with black triangles interspersed. The toilet sat next to a radiator, beneath the slightly opened bathroom window. The smell of perfumed soaps permeated the room, and the fluffy red and white towels invited him to shower off the sweat he had developed during his sleep.

Downstairs, Austin had just arrived home from a long day at the newspaper. Though he was a bit tired, he was excited about the evening with their houseguest.

"Hi, Austin," Sara said from the kitchen.

"Hi, honey," Austin said as he walked into the big country kitchen. "Smells great in here."

"That's the bread you smell. It turned out fantastically. Here, try a piece."

He took a piece and tasted it. That is outstanding, dear. I can't wait for supper. How long will it be?" he asked.

"Probably within the hour. We're still waiting for Marlena to come home, which should be any minute now. I don't want to start poaching the fish until everyone is here."

"Where is Adam?"

"He's still upstairs. He was taking a nap, but I think I heard him go into the guest bathroom to take a shower. He'll probably be down shortly," she said.

"Okay, I'm going up to change into something a little more comfortable."

"Not too comfortable, Austin, we do have a guest. We want to make a positive impression."

"Yes, dear. I'll dress accordingly."

Marlena came through the front entrance with a burst of energy.

"I'm home," she cried.

Sara called for her to come into the kitchen, which she promptly did.

"Mom, that bread smells wonderful!" she exclaimed. "What kind is it?"

"Oh, it's just some random recipe I found in one of the cookbooks. It really is quite good."

Marlena hastily tore a piece off of the broken end and tossed it into her mouth. "This is great, Mom. I went to the market and got the salad stuff you asked for. Do you want me to make it?"

"Yes, then you might want to go and freshen up."

Marlena finished helping her mom in the kitchen, then left to go upstairs. As she bounded up the spiral walnut staircase, she looked up to see Adam on his way down. She smiled. "Good evening, Mr. Freeman. How was your sleep?"

"Oh, hi. I slept fine, thanks."

As they passed each other on the wide staircase, their eyes locked. Marlena again flashed Adam an enchanting smile. He stumbled down the next couple of stairs, and his misstep made a loud thump heard all through the house.

"What happened?" Sara said. "Is everyone alright?"

Adam, embarrassed by the whole scene, stammered, "Uh, well…"

"Yeah, everything's okay, we just stumbled on this darn loose carpet on the staircase," Marlena quickly piped in.

"Austin, I told you to get that thing fixed a week ago,"

Adam sheepishly smiled a thank you to Marlena and she obliged with a devilish smirk. The two continued on their separate ways.

10.

The kitchen was filled with the aroma of freshly baked bread, steaming vegetables, and the sweet, pungent smell of redfish poaching in white wine, garlic, and fresh herbs. Everyone had converged to the kitchen area, eager to help get this feast to the dining room table.

Marlena was busy setting the table, while her dad went to the cellar to pick out a couple of bottles of wine to accompany the meal. He looked over his selection and decided two bottles of DeLoach O.F.S. chardonnay. This ought to do it, he thought to himself. He then returned to the kitchen to join the gathering.

Unable to find anything helpful to do in the kitchen, Adam went out to the backyard. He walked back in just as everything was in place.

Adam offered an assortment of freshly picked wildflowers. "I thought these might be nice for the table. I hope you don't mind me picking them?"

"Oh, Adam, how sweet. They are absolutely beautiful. Mind? Maybe you should take Austin with you and show him where you found them. I think we're a little overdue with the romantic gestures around here. Right, Austin?" Sara smiled at her husband and winked to assure him she was just having a bit of fun.

Austin smiled.

Sara went and got a vase and then placed the colorful bouquet on the dining room table.

Austin raised his arms, motioning everyone toward the table.

"Let's be seated. Everything looks great, except possibly my image, thanks to you, Adam," Austin joked.

Adam smirked and apologized, quickly realizing no harm was done. Everyone took a seat and Austin immediately began filling wine glasses with the special chardonnay he had chosen from the cellar. After everyone was served, Austin raised his glass to make a toast.

"Here's to new friends, new opportunities, and a new consciousness that will invoke kindness and compassion in the hearts of all people, for all people. Adam, although we don't necessarily feel good about the circumstances under which you came to be here today, we are very happy you are sharing this wonderful meal with us. Welcome!"

"Well said, dear," Sara said.

"I agree. Good job, Dad," Marlena said.

"Those are very kind words, Mr. Thompson. I really don't know what I did to deserve them. Thank you."

"Well everyone, let's eat," Austin exclaimed.

"Here, here," Marlena said, raising her glass.

Everyone began eating.

"Mom, I love this bread. You have to show me where the recipe is," Marlena remarked.

"Mrs. Thompson,"Adam added, "I have never tasted fish prepared like this. This is truly the best meal I've had in quite some time."

Austin just kept on eating and grumbled, "Umm!"

"Thank you all for your compliments, including your grunts, dear. I take them to mean you're enjoying yourself immensely. Oh and by the way, Austin, this wine is excellent."

"No honey, it's Out F—-ing Standing," Austin replied.

"I beg your pardon, Austin!" the startled Sara cried.

Austin quickly explained, "It's the name of the chardonnay, Sara. DeLoach, O.F.S. According to the wine merchant, who heard it directly from the wine maker, O.F.S. stands for Out F—-ing Standing."

"How interesting," Sara responded, still somewhat embarrassed.

Marlena playfully added, "Well, dad, I agree with the wine maker, this wine is Out F—"

"Marlena! We do have a guest," Sara asserted with a firm tone.

The group then broke into laughter over Marlena's defiance. The tone was light and the conversation easy. By the time the meal was finished, everyone was relaxed with one another. Sara cleared the table and, with Marlena's help, served each person a slice of chocolate walnut torte with a scoop of vanilla ice cream and coffee.

Adam was thankful for the Thompsons' hospitality. They were genuinely kind and benevolent people. Something was bothering him, though. He wondered why these wonderful people were living in a town that initially seemed so hateful and backward. Lost in his thoughts, Adam drifted from the conversation.

"Adam, what are you thinking about?"

A bit startled, he said, "Oh, nothing really." He paused for a moment. "Well, truthfully, I was just wondering why such kind people would end up in a town like this." He looked around the table and waited for a response.

Almost as if choreographed, each one of the Thompsons simultaneously took a deep breath and let out a sigh.

"Well, who wants to take this one?" Sara asked.

"Dad, why don't you start?" Marlena suggested.

"Why don't I?" Austin said. "Where shall I begin? Well, Adam, before we moved to Eve, I owned a reputable and very influential publication in White Plains, New York. I had spent the majority of my adult life in publishing and had become pretty good at it. We lived in an ideal town that had everything to offer—a great school system for our daughter, no crime, everyone was supportive and friendly, and we were close enough to New York City that if we wanted to go to a museum or see a play we could plan a day to drive over and be entertained. Everything was perfect."

Adam could sense this whole story was not a very comfortable one for the Thompsons, especially Austin. "You don't have to go on, Mr Thompson."

"Oh, it's okay. Well, in a span of approximately six months, White Plains became the home to four other publications, two of which were national, and one had an international circulation with a billionaire backing it.

"The first thing that happened was that, within a short period of time, I lost most, if not all, of my key staff to the three larger publications. Then my niche in the marketplace got gobbled up because the mega publications began expanding their markets into mine. With my former staff on their payrolls, they knew exactly how to go about it.

"To make a long story short, before I was completely forced out of business, I was tendered a fairly reasonable offer to sell, which I did. It seemed almost kind of them to make me the type of offer they did, considering how the publication had been devalued.

At that point the paper was probably not worth what they gave me for it. On the other hand, it was probably worth five times as much two years earlier. Such is life."

He paused for a moment. "Anyway, I had to find something to invest the money in or take a huge capital gains hit. The only promising publication available for sale in the country at the time was the *EveExaminer.* So, we bought it and here we are. Of course, I've made some other investments with the cash that was left over, and we bought this beautiful, old house, which we all love. Basically, as far as the publishing industry is concerned, Eve was the only town that held any promise. For the most part, we've learned how to deal with or avoid undesirable circumstances."

"Although I don't necessarily concur with Austin's last statement, that is basically our story," Sara commented. "I might also add that before we moved to Eve, I worked in social services doing career planning and crisis intervention work in and around New York. It was something I found very rewarding, but I don't miss the stress. That was before I became a docile housewife."

"Well, that's a very interesting story. I'm sorry to hear about your newspaper. It sounds like it meant a lot to you," Adam said.

"How about you, Adam? We know how you came to be in Eve, but tell us about your background," Sara said.

Marlena's interest picked up as the conversation shifted to Adam. She listened as she took a bite of her dessert. Adam was seated on her right, and she glanced at him out of the corner of her eye as she slowly pulled the fork from her mouth.

Adam took a deep breath and let out a sigh. "Well, let me see. I'm originally from Detroit. The area where I grew up was a nice, middle-class, Jewish neighborhood when we moved there in the early sixties. We were the only black family within about a mile radius. By the time I reached high school, that same neighborhood had become a ghetto. I never got into any gang activities or anything like that. I did, however, develop a penchant for surviving in the streets. The guys I hung out with were all into sports and athletics. Well, some of us…them…were into chasing girls, too. Nonetheless, it was all pretty harmless stuff. None of the violent stuff the gangs were into.

"Since my friends and I were into sports, we were always either coming from or going to a game. We frequently ran in a pack. I don't know if we thought about it then, but if you would have seen us together, you probably would have taken us for a gang. The way we traveled together probably served as a pretty good deterrent from getting attacked by one of the gangs in the area. It probably also scared a few people who thought we were a gang. Anyway, I ended up playing football for my high school team, the Mumford Mustangs."

"That name sounds familiar," Austin said.

"Yeah, maybe because it was the school T-shirt Eddie Murphy wore in the first *Beverly Hills Cop* movie," Adam responded.

"Oh, yeah, that's right, I remember that," Marlena said. "So that's your high school. We really do have a celebrity among us." She gave Adam a playful smile, which he returned.

"What position did you play?" Austin asked.

"I went both ways. I played wide out on offense as well as backup quarterback. On defense I played free safety. The summer before my senior year, *Parade* magazine had me projected as a second-team, all-American split end—best in the Midwest. Colleges everywhere wanted me to take a look at their campuses. I had my heart set on the University of Michigan, since I had wanted to wear one of those winged helmets from the time I was a little kid. When I was in my senior year in high school, the season started and the first four games went as well as I could have ever imagined. I had ten touchdown receptions and another two touchdown returns off of interceptions. Boy, was I on top of the world."

He stopped, looking down at the table, then took a deep breath. "That week after practice some friends and I were walking home past this little restaurant and some guys came running out. Suddenly gunshots started raining, it seemed from every direction. I hit the ground, like everyone else, but as I landed on the pavement I felt a surge of heat run through my right knee. When I looked down at it, it was shattered. I was bleeding all over the place and it didn't seem like it was going to stop. It stopped bleeding some hours later in the emergency room at Providence Hospital. It also stopped any hopes of me being able to afford going to college and living my football dreams in that maize and blue uniform."

Everyone in the room was quiet for a moment.

"How sad, Adam," Sara finally said.

Adam, rather embarrassed, mumbled, "This is really kind of a long, boring story..."

"Adam, please go on," Austin said. "You have a very interesting story. We want to hear the rest of it."

"Okay, well let me see. After that I just kind of lost my mind. Not literally, of course, or maybe I did. I stopped going to class regularly and started hanging out with some pretty seedy characters at school. With the way my grades went down, I barely hung on to graduate. I guess I was a little depressed."

"I bet!" Sara said.

"My brother ended up convincing me to attend the community college he worked at as a counselor. So, I began to reestablish myself academically. I also got a job at Detroit City Airport, refueling planes. A glorified gas station attendant, so to speak. It's funny, because I remember being fascinated by airplanes as a kid, but being black and poor, I never really thought of it as a serious option. It may seem kind of silly, but that's how I felt, until I met a guy named Buck—Buck Taylor.

"Buck would fly into City Airport in his Beechcraft, King Air. Boy, was that a beautiful airplane. He was the first black pilot I even knew existed. He would tell me stories of his old war days flying with the Tuskeegee Airmen. He had a way of making it seem exciting. Finally, Buck convinced me I should give flying a try. He took me up one day in the right front seat of his plane. Boy, that was it. He let me execute the takeoff and at the precise moment the wheels pulled off of the ground, I was hooked.

"Buck referred me to University Air Academy, an airline-sponsored university in Idaho. He pulled a few strings and arranged for Tuskegee Airman grants, and there I was learning to fly 737s and DC-8s. You just never know. So, I ended up channeling my all-American football energy into flying and graduated third out of a class of one hundred and eighty five. I was also one of only two blacks to graduate in that class. I started to feel pride in myself and a sense of purpose that may have been as exhilarating as the flying itself.

"I can imagine," Austin said, nodding.

"I flew for United for a few years until I received an offer to fly Lee Iacocca's Cessna Citation at twice what I was making at United. That was such a thrill. I got a chance to meet some very influential people and fly all over the world. That's what I did until just recently. Now I am trying to find my way up to Washington State to buy a small FBO in Friday Harbor. That is where I was headed when I landed in that field. Basically, that's my life in a nutshell—albeit a long nutshell. Forgive me for rambling."

"Oh no, Adam, not at all," Sara said. "You've led a very fascinating life. I don't think I've ever met anyone who has been through the types of circumstances you have and prevailed so strongly. I'm sure you will become an inspiration to many some day."

"I'll say," Austin added.

Marlena just sat there staring at Adam with a twinkle in her eyes. "Mr. Freeman, you are a very impressive man, to say the least. Could I convince you to come and talk to my second-grade class? It won't take long. I would be honored and it would do some of these children wonders to meet a man who has accomplished what you have." She looked at him with an earnest gaze. "Please, Mr. Freeman, if you have the time, would you give it some thought?"

Adam was thinking to himself that he would do anything to be able to spend more time with this beautiful woman, and here she was begging him to come to her job. God was alive, he thought as he smiled back at Marlena. "Sure, I'd be happy to."

They returned to small talk and everyone helped clear the remaining dishes from the dining room table. Austin and Sara excused themselves and retired to their bedroom for the evening.

Marlena asked Adam if he'd been given the tour of the grounds. Although he had walked around earlier, he said he hadn't. Marlena motioned Adam to follow her out the front door. Adam had a feeling of nervous excitement. His heart was racing and he had butterflies in his stomach. He wanted to believe Marlena was as attracted to him as he was to her, but the childhood perceptions of himself were so embedded he couldn't see this radiant, young, white woman seeing him as anything more than a passing fancy.

He tried to let go of the past and followed Marlena outside. At the same time he tried not to read anything more into it than she was giving him a tour as a friendly gesture.

The night sky was one of resplendent grace. The three-quarter moon shone brightly, along with a billion magnificent twinkling stars. It would be hard for even the most natural of enemies to continue a quarrel under these circumstances. They both stood there for a moment, soaking it up.

"What a beautiful night," Adam said.

Marlena, still looking up at the stars, simply stated, "Magical!"

The two stood there silently for a few moments.

Adam was the first to break the silence. "So, Marlena, you really didn't get a chance to say much about yourself during dinner. What's your story?"

Marlena thought for a moment. "My story, let me see. I guess you got a lot of the background information from my dad. I grew up in White Plains, mostly. We did, however, make temporary residences in other places—San Francisco for awhile, I lived in Australia for a year, and Vancouver for about eighteen months. Other than all of the travel, I guess you would say I had a rather normal upbringing, if there is such a thing."

He laughed softly.

"I was taken with my mom's passion for civil liberties. I remember traveling to the city with her as a child. She worked in social services and would do counseling with single mothers and other people who had fallen on misfortune. Mostly, the misfortune of being raised in a culture that cares very little about those who aren't represented by a major lobbyist in Washington."

Adam nodded.

"During that time, I realized I too wanted to do something to help others. I saw my mom's position had a purpose and a very valuable one at that. Somehow I wanted to get closer to the core of the solution, which is why I chose teaching. My dad is still a bit disappointed in my decision because he feels my talents could be better utilized in publishing or on Wall Street, at least from a financial standpoint. Or maybe as a lawyer or foreign emissary. I realize I probably could do better monetarily in another field. What's most meaningful for me is sharing my knowledge with children and helping them to explore their own minds. When that happens, time stands still. There's no other place I could ever imagine wanting to be."

"That kind of sentiment is hard to find," Adam said.

Marlena nodded. "For now, at least, I'm sure I'm in the right place, doing the right thing. Eve is so filled with fear and hatred. I feel like I need to be here now—to make a difference in these children's futures. I have an opportunity to subtly counter some predominant beliefs in this community, such as the whole notion of segregation and how neither side feels it can trust the other.

"These kids are getting this type of message before they can even speak. I have been reprimanded more than once for my little lessons on compassion for fellow beings, regardless of race or religion. For some reason I believe this town, as hateful as it is, is ripe for a shift in its thinking. That's why I don't let up. It may appear that way at times, but that is by design. I need to remain in the good graces of this community, if I am to accomplish what I have set out to do."

Adam, impressed by Marlena's perspective, said, "It seems like you have developed your own little covert operation against racism and hatred."

"I have. It isn't an obsession, though, it's just what I feel I have been directed to do."

"It sounds wonderful," Adam added, "You are a pretty phenomenal young woman. You are so clear about what you are supposed to be doing. You seem to have your life pretty well mapped out."

"Well, I don't know about being all planned out but I do know what I'm supposed to be doing right now, or I did."

Her open-ended statement seemed harmless enough, but definitely implied something deeper. She flashed Adam a sly grin but he didn't catch on. He just smiled back. "So, where did you go to school?"

Marlena thought for a moment. "Well, pretty much all over. I have always loved to travel, so early on I decided I would do a part of my studies abroad. My junior year in high school I spent in Moscow. When I graduated from high school I attended Yale for a year and then went back overseas. I lived with an English family in Zimbabwe. Being immersed in a culture so unlike our own was one of the wildest experiences of my life. Anyway, I returned to the states and finished my undergraduate degree at Syracuse. I spent a year in law school until I realized how sleazy everyone was and decided to get my teaching certificate and here I am. I originally moved down here to help dad get things going at the *Examiner*, but something happened while I was here and I got the message that this is where I had some meaningful work to do."

"That is a pretty incredible story," Adam said. He felt emotions for Marlena he had never felt for anyone. Her outer beauty aroused passion in him and he could think of nothing but spending the rest of his life with her.

She was a gift he never could have conceived of until this moment and here she was, a dream made manifest. He could not, however, shake the chains of his misconceptions of himself. The feeling that he really didn't have much to offer her in a long-term relationship dogged his thoughts.

All he had to hope for was the chance that she, too, felt a physical attraction. Maybe he could share a part of her soul through a physical connection. He felt he could cherish that for a lifetime, whether or not the connection lasted.

They walked around the back side of the porch and eventually worked their way to the edge of the Thompson's four-acre lot.

Adam turned to Marlena. "Don't you get tired of the conflict around here? Don't you ever crave to be in a place that's more at ease?"

She looked up at him. "Sure, sometimes, but like I said, it's very clear to me where I should be right now."

"You, must have a boyfriend or someone special here then?" he said, immediately feeling awkward for having done so.

Smiling, she said, "Well, that would be yes and no. I am seeing someone here, but we are more friends than lovers. His name is Brad and he is kind of the town hero. He was a football star in high school, like yourself, and brought Eve its only state title when he played about six or seven years ago. Brad is a nice guy, he's just not the type of man I ultimately want to fall in love with. It does get a bit lonely in this town, and Brad is always there to show me a good time."

Adam nodded, but said nothing.

"It's a pretty harmless relationship. Of course, everyone in town would like to see us married off and with hundreds of little Brad football studs running around. It's almost like a miniature version of the Nazis' master race idea, which is not all that surprising around here. So, there it is, Mr. Freeman. That's my story. What about you? Anyone special?"

Adam was taken off guard by the question. At first he chuckled, and then let out a sigh. "Well, I did have someone special, I thought, until I got here."

"What do you mean?"

Gazing into the dark, star-speckled sky, he replied, "When I woke up in the clinic Tuesday, I began making calls back home. The first call I made was to my girlfriend, Donna. It was seven o'clock in the morning and a man answered the phone. He sounded like he had just woken up. Donna started making lame excuses, but I knew she was lying. She has done this before, and I have given her the benefit of the doubt. I thought it was partly my fault for being gone so much. That had something to do with why I wanted to buy the FBO in Friday Harbor—to try and create a more stable personal life. I thought maybe she would be a part of it, but I guess not."

Marlena hugged him. "Adam, you poor guy. You are having one heck of a week aren't you."

"Yeah, one heck of a week!"

Looking back up at him, she smiled. "Adam, how tall are you?"

"How tall am I? I'm six-four," he responded proudly.

"That's tall," she said.

"Well, how tall are you?"

"I'm only five-three, and I wish I were taller."

"Taller! Why? You are absolutely perfect." He looked down at her smiling and admiring every inch of her five-foot, three-inch frame.

If he had ever seen a woman put together as well as she was, he couldn't remember. It wasn't just that she was a stunningly perfect image to behold, although that's what started it all. She also had a brilliant spirit that came through every word she said. Adam felt God was talking through her.

This was the first person Adam had experienced as a living child of God. Ironically, she had not mentioned religion once. He knew deep inside he loved this woman, and the thought terrified him, because he also felt she could never truly be his.

They walked to the white porch swing at the back of the house and sat down. They began to gently swing back and forth, looking out into the night sky. A shooting star flashed across the sky and at the same time they said, "Did you see...?" Both stopped and giggled.

Marlena then told Adam, "Close your eyes and make a wish." She closed her eyes and made one, too.

After a few moments they opened their eyes and looked at each other. Their gaze was a lingering one. It was as if each was trying to look into the other's heart to see what it would say.

"What did you wish for?" Marlena quietly asked Adam.

Looking into her eyes, he answered in the same quiet tone, "Isn't that bad luck? What did you wish for?"

Marlena sat silent for a moment, holding his gaze. She leaned closer, looking into his brown eyes. She could feel his breath blowing gently against her lips and she kissed him. They held the kiss for just a moment, but its effect was unmistakable. She leaned even closer to him and whispered into his ear, "That."

Adam, a bit confused, looked into her eyes. "That?"

She smiled. "That was what I wished for."

11.

Adam stood in front of a class of twenty or so third graders talking about the basics of flight. Their little minds were focused on every word he was saying. All eyes were fixed on his hand drawing an airplane on the blackboard as he went on about lift, drag, weight, and thrust.

As amazed as these children were by the information being offered, they were even more amazed by its source. The four black children in the class were brimming with pride that one of their own was able to fly an airplane. They felt even more fortunate that they got to meet him. Their feelings were probably similar to those of Blacks in the early fifties who witnessed Jackie Robinson becoming the first black, professional, baseball player. To see him in person must have seemed like seeing Christ Jesus in the flesh—an honor to behold and cherish for all time.

As for the white children, they too were amazed by this tall, brown, dignified-looking man giving a technical presentation. All of their lives they'd been taught that Negroes weren't to be trusted and were dim-witted, even if it didn't seem that way. Under no circumstances would a Negro have the innate intelligence required to learn all that was required to perform a task as complex as flying an airplane.

Marlena was the first white they had encountered that challenged these notions. She had found ways to do it subtly, so as not to be prematurely silenced in her efforts to make a difference. Adam was truly a triumph in her quest to make Eve a more nurturing community for everyone, black and white.

He was perfect—intelligent, articulate, expressive, and very presentable. The bottom line was that she found him drop-dead gorgeous. He could easily have been mistaken for a professional football or basketball player. In any case, Marlena felt Adam had been sent to her from heaven, and not just for one reason. Not only was he the epitome of what a black person could accomplish in the right circumstances, but she loved him.

The previous evening had affected her deeply. For the first time, all of the passion she felt for the betterment of the planet had shifted. Now she felt that the mere act of being with Adam helped to make the world a better place. How could it not be so, with the love she felt pouring from her heart?

Marlena found herself only catching parts of Adam's presentation on introduction to flight. Her mind drifted back and forth between what was going on in her classroom and the visions she had about spending time with this remarkable man. She remembered last night's kiss and it made her heart smile. Anticipating the next time it would happen, she got butterflies in her stomach.

"...and that is the first lesson in the principles of flight. If there are any questions, I'll be happy to answer them now."

One of the boys raised his hand. When Adam called on him he asked, "How fast do you go when you fly?"

Adam smiled and chuckled, saying, "I knew this question would come up. It was one of the first things I asked, too. It's hard to give a definite answer. It depends on the plane, how long of a flight I'm taking, my altitude or how high up I am, even the weather is a factor, particularly the wind. I'll just tell you this—if I were to fly from Eve to Seattle... does anyone know where Seattle is?"

Marlena walked over next to the blackboard and pulled down a map of the United States. "Who would like to show the class where Seattle, Washington is?" She said.

A little girl anxiously raised her hand. Marlena motioned the little girl forward and she jumped from her seat, walked to the map, and confidently pointed to precisely the spot on the map marked as Puget Sound.

"That's right, very good," Adam exclaimed.

When the little one had returned to her seat, Adam continued, "Seattle is approximately 2000 miles away from where we are. So, if I were to fly my Malibu from here to there, I would choose an altitude of around twenty-thousand feet and fly at a speed of maybe 210 knots. That would be about 240 miles per hour."

"Wow," came the collective response from the class. One child added, "That's fast!"

"Well, that is pretty fast," Adam said. "However, my little Malibu is a tortoise compared to the airplanes I fly for other people. Private jets typically fly over six hundred miles per hour."

Again, a collective, "Wow."

Then a girl raised her hand. "Where is your favorite place to go—to fly to, I mean?"

Adam thought for a moment, holding his chin. "That's a good question. Well, up until a few days ago my favorite place was Spain or Seattle." He looked over at Marlena. "But, you know, I've found there are some pretty wonderful things to be found wherever you go, especially here in Eve."

Marlena felt a surge of emotion run through her. Had it not been for being in the classroom, she would have acted on the feelings in an instant. Instead, she downplayed them and offered a cordial, "What kind words, Mr. Freeman. Thank you." Her thoughts, however, were focused on being alone with him again.

Their eyes locked as they smiled at each other.

"Mr. Freeman, how do you get to be a black pilot?" A little boy said.

Adam looked over at the little colored boy and there was snickering throughout the classroom, which Marlena quickly hushed.

The boy wore a tattered T-shirt and he looked unkempt. Adam looked directly into the boy's eyes and said, "Son, what is your name?"

"Ricky," the boy responded in a heavy southern drawl.

"Ricky, one day I decided what I wanted to do in life was to fly airplanes. On that day I also decided no one in the world was going to keep me from doing just that. A man named Buck pointed me in the right direction and gave me a start, and from then on it just took work, work, and more work. When times got hard, I just resolved to never give up. You know, Ricky, I was no different than you are when I was a kid. If you want to be a pilot, you can. I'll help you, but there is one thing that you must always remember. You won't be a black pilot, you will be a great pilot, as well as a great man."

Adam's eyes began to fill with tears, and he turned around as if to wipe the notes from the blackboard and quickly brushed the tear from his eye. He turned back around and thanked the class for inviting him to share his experience.

Marlena excused herself from the class and walked Adam out into the hallway. She told Adam her day of work was almost done because of a scheduled half-day and that she would be honored if she could buy him lunch. He graciously accepted and they arranged to meet in front of the elementary school so they could walk to the diner together.

She reached up and gave Adam a kiss on the cheek and thanked him for the beautiful talk he had given her class. As he walked down the hall, Marlena stood there watching him go. She held her hands together over her heart, wondering if this could be real.

12.

The school bell rang and the sound of children's excitement filled the air. Their little voices squealed as they ran out the front door of the school building in anticipation of an extended day of after-school mischief. Adam sat on the right side of the school building's concrete slab porch. As the children rushed by, he smiled at some he recognized from the talk he had given earlier in the day.

Looking at the children, he reflected back on his own childhood and began to feel thankful for what he'd been able to accomplish in his lifetime. He noticed the little boy coming in his direction whose question had touched him so that morning. "Ricky, right?"

The boy smiled "You remembered."

"Ricky," Adam continued, "I don't think I will ever forget you. Especially since I'll be teaching you how to fly. You're going to be my first student."

"Wow, really? Thanks, Mr. Freeman," Ricky said excitedly.

Marlena walked up and greeted the two of them, "Well, it looks like the two of you are getting along."

"Yes, ma'am," Ricky said.

Adam just smiled and nodded.

"Well, Ricky you better run along home now," Marlena said. "Mr. Freeman and I have some important things to talk about."

Ricky looked up at them and said good-bye. His face filled with both a newfound hope and the sadness of having to leave his new friend so suddenly.

Standing at the top of the stairs to the school were two, middle- aged women, both with obvious looks of disgust on their faces. One of the women turned to the other and snidely commented, "That's him. I actually saw her kiss that nigger in the hallway by her classroom. It was absolutely disgusting."

The other woman chimed in, "And to think she's responsible for the little ones. What do you think she's teaching them?"

The two women continued to stare at them.

Ignoring the women's remarks, Marlena grabbed Adam's hand and pulled him up from his seated position. "Come on," she said. "let's get out of here. The cafe is just a short walk, and we can get a bite to eat there."

They began to walk away from the school building, and as they did, she asked him what he thought of her students.

"I think you have a wonderful class. You have done a wonderful job with those kids. Tell me more about Ricky."

"Ricky is a great kid. He is different, though. His communication and reading skills are pretty low, but in math and subjects where he gets to create he excels, almost bordering on genius. The other kids just hear the way he speaks and assume he's stupid, so he has a very difficult time socially. Even some of his other teachers ridicule him. He just needs some extra attention and he'll be fine. The problem is, I don't always have the extra time to give him, and I'm sure he gets very little support at home."

Adam's curiosity was piqued. "What do you mean?"

"Well, his mom is a known alcoholic and she pretty much neglects him. She is so wrapped up in her own pain she doesn't have a clue how much her little boy is suffering. I was just explaining to my parents that every time I offer any assistance, she shuns me. I think she feels like I am trying to steal him away from her or something. It's a pretty sad situation, but you know, I think today may have been a turning point. Thanks to a wonderful man named Adam Freeman."

He shrugged. "Well, I hope so. I saw a lot of myself in that kid. I hope I was able to do him some good. I really tried to make a difference. It's too bad I won't be here longer."

They continued walking, oblivious of the stares they were receiving from passersby. Whites didn't fraternize with blacks in Eve. The few that did kept it carefully hidden, so as not to provoke any harm to themselves from the locals. Downtown Eve, with its nostalgic storefronts, was definitely a buzz this afternoon.

The couple arrived in front of the Eve Eatery. Marlena turned toward Adam and told him she didn't know exactly what to expect, but that this place was pretty calm, generally speaking. What she was insinuating was that she didn't expect any racially inspired problems to occur because they were together.

As they entered the restaurant, the occupants at every table turned and looked at them, startled. They heard a bit of murmuring coming from a couple of the tables further back. There were about thirty people scattered around a dozen tables in the diner. The place looked like something out of a seventies sitcom. The waitresses wore pink outfits with white aprons. On top of the lunch counter were stainless steel platform cake holders with clear plastic tops.

Adam noticed two middle-aged black men sitting at a table as he and Marlena walked toward the back of the room. His eyes met theirs and they nodded at each other in recognition. The two black men seemed amazed at what they were seeing. They also looked very concerned, as if they saw a grand piano swinging above Adam's head and were wondering when it was going to drop.

The couple walked past the stares and found a table halfway back on the right wall, under a picture of Elvis. Not far away, Adam also noticed a very attractive young black woman sitting alone sipping coffee, reading a thick textbook. He couldn't make out the title, but couldn't recall seeing a textbook that thick since his sophomore year at UAA in Idaho.

One of the waitresses came over and took Adam's and Marlena's order. Then curtly turned and walked away from the table. Marlena looked over at Adam and shrugged.

They sat across the table, just staring at each other. As they did, they got lost in each other's eyes. It was as if each of them could look into the other's heart and feel the love they shared. It seemed like a love that had been there forever, just waiting for the other to arrive and take their proper place.

They started talking about how Adam was going to get his aircraft fixed.

"My regular mechanic can't come, but he gave me the name of a good mechanic who can fly down from St. Louis. It'll be airborne again fairly soon, I hope."

His main concern was how thoroughly the FAA and NTSB were going to need to investigate his aircraft after the accident. Both agencies were sending investigators down to inspect the crash site and his aircraft. The preliminary findings had put Adam pretty much in the clear, as far as his actions as a pilot were concerned. It was unclear, however, whether Alpha Lima would be grounded until its airframe, engine, and mechanical systems were put through a detailed inspection by the agencies' safety engineers. If that turned out to be the case, it could take a couple of weeks after the repairs were completed to get out of there.

"I'll do whatever I can to help you, Adam. Feel free to ask—anything." Marlena said.

When they finished eating, Adam ordered a slice of Dutch apple pie with vanilla ice cream and a cup of coffee.

"I've got some things to take care of back in my classroom, but would you come by the school in about an hour so we can drive home together?" Marlena said.

Adam was thrilled by the proposition and eagerly accepted.

Marlena grabbed the bill. "I'll have them put your dessert on it as well. Thanks again for sharing your experiences with my class. You really are one of the most impressive people I've ever met."

Adam, wallowing in his insecurities, told himself she was just being nice. It was hard for him to imagine that in all of her worldly experiences, he was one of the most impressive people she had ever met. Nonetheless, her kind gesture struck a chord. He looked up at her as she turned to walk away.

"Marlena…"

She turned and smiled at him.

As he tried to formulate what he would say to her, his heart pounded furiously. It was like he had just run a hundred-yard sprint. As he began to speak, he realized the people in close proximity would hear him, so, instead of revealing his deepest feelings, he retreated. "You know, I want to go and find the man who pulled me from my aircraft, Sam, and thank him."

Marlena, smiled, touched by his thoughtfulness. "It is probably a good idea for you to meet old Sam. I don't know much about him, but I do think he did a remarkable thing. Be sure to thank him for delivering you to our doorstep that night, will ya?" She winked and gave him a devilishly sexy grin. "Do you know how to get to his place?"

"Well, I think I was on his property when I went by the plane to get my things. I saw an old house about a half-mile from where I put down. I think I'll be okay finding it. If not, I'll come and get you to help me."

"I'll see you in about an hour, right?" Marlena said as she smiled and walked away.

Adam's eyes followed Marlena as she left the cafe. A tall, athletic-looking fellow greeted her once she was outside. Adam noticed the two of them smile at each other and then embrace. It seemed harmless enough, but Adam realized everything was too good to be true. That was probably her lover. His joy quickly turned to disappointment. He lowered his head and stared into his plate of dessert.

13.

"Hi, my name is Teri. Teri Jones. You must be Adam," the woman said as she extended her hand.

A bit startled, Adam looked up from the pie he was eating and smiled at the attractive black woman. His mouth was full of pie and ice cream. He put down his fork and shook her hand, still unable to speak. He quickly chewed and swallowed his food to respond.

He stood and began to speak, stammering a bit. "Hello.

Uh, yes, I am Adam. Adam Freeman. It's very nice to meet you, Ms. Jones."

"Teri," she insisted.

"Yes, of course, Teri. How do you know who I am? Or, in a town this size, is that a dumb question?"

"Well, this town is pretty small. Not much goes on here without everyone finding out about it."

As the woman spoke, Adam detected a southern accent, but her speech was not slow and dull. She was, in fact, quite articulate. She was also very neat, wearing understated attire. She wore a sleeveless, pale-yellow sundress and white sandals. Her complexion was almost identical to his—deep, caramel brown. She had dark eyebrows and long black hair that was pulled back in a ponytail. They could have almost passed for brother and sister.

"So, you're a pilot, huh? I don't think anyone around here has ever seen a black pilot in person before. I heard about your accident. Are you all right?" she asked with concern.

"Yes, I'm okay. I bruised some ribs, but it's nothing serious. Excuse me for being rude. Would you like to join me?" Adam motioned for her to sit down at the table.

"Well, I wouldn't want to interrupt anything," she said, looking toward the seat Marlena had occupied during lunch.

Adam was puzzled for a moment, then realized what she was implying. "You mean Marlena? She had to go back to work. There isn't any problem with you sitting there. Please, have a seat," he said with a little smirk.

He leaned over and pulled the seat out. She sat and gave him a coy smile. The look she gave him was fairly reassuring—a look of pleasant but reluctant understanding.

"I really don't have long," Teri explained. "I have to go to class."

There was a moment of silence and Adam returned to finishing his pie.

Teri looked at him. "So, how do you like flying?"

"I love it! Flying is unlike anything I've ever experienced. You get a sense of freedom at thirty thousand feet you can't get anywhere else. At least not anyplace I've been. It's really a wonderful experience."

She smiled at his enthusiasm. "Do you ever get scared?"

Although a smile came to his face, it was more an indication of discomfort than amusement. He slowly raised the last morsel of pie to his mouth and continued to stare at the melted ice cream on the plate. After a few moments of swirling his fork in the melted ice cream, he looked up. "Not until a couple of days ago. The way I arrived in your fair town was quite an experience, and it hasn't let up yet. I mean with the Klan running around throwing bricks through clinic windows and all. I'm not used to treatment that is that blatant. Where I come from bigotry is a bit more subtle. Not enough to kill you, just enough to make you feel a little less than human. I guess I can deal with that 'cause I'm used to it."

"Well, Mr. Freeman, you seem to have found a way around the racism and have done pretty well for yourself," Teri said. "You fly planes for a living, right?"

"Well, yes, at the moment I do fly for a living."

"What do you mean, at the moment?"

"Well, when my plane went down I was on my way to Washington to look at a small airport whose primary fixed-base operation or FBO, is for sale. I'd like to have my own light aircraft operation, and this prospect seems pretty promising. That is, if I can get airborne fairly quickly and get up there."

"So, in essence, what you're telling me is that you're looking to buy your own airline, right?" said Teri, impressed.

Realizing he had more explaining to do, Adam remarked, "Well, sort of. It's more like I would be running a flight center that provides services to other pilots. For instance, we would offer fuel and tie-down services for pilots traveling to our area. In addition, we would offer flight instruction, access to phones and computers for flight planning and preparation, pilot supplies such as charts, flight guides, headsets, flight computers and so on. We would also offer private charters for local business travelers and scenic flights around the islands for tourists. Puget Sound is an incredibly beautiful area, especially from the air. I was even thinking about adding a restaurant with a view of the runway to make the airport more of an attraction for local pilots."

"It sounds like you've got everything planned out pretty well, Mr. Freeman. How about Mrs. Right? Was she planned for already? Maybe I should have said Mrs. White."

Even though the tone of Teri's voice was not bitter, her statements cut into his heart like a cold stiletto. He felt as if he had betrayed the entire black race by falling for Marlena. He hadn't even been on a real date with her yet, but from the way he responded, the depth of his feelings became quite clear to him. Somehow he managed to hide his emotions and coolly address Teri's remark.

"No, there is not a provision for Mrs. Right—or White, as you put it—at this time. I just had my heart broken, but that is a whole other discussion and you have a class to attend," Adam responded somewhat curtly.

"Reverend Jacobson tells me you'll be at the First Baptist on Sunday. I do hope I'll see you there." As she stood to leave, Teri smiled invitingly at Adam. She then walked over to him and reached out her hand. He stood up and shook her hand then, out of nowhere, she reached up and kissed him on the cheek.

"I wouldn't make any plans for Mrs. Right just yet," she said as she turned and walked out of the cafe. Adam watched her leave, half in a daze. Rarely had he felt as perplexed as he did at that moment.

Adam took a sip of his water and looked up at the ceiling as if to ask for divine guidance. Then he walked out of the little cafe and headed back to pick up Marlena in front of the school building, as they had previously arranged. She wasn't there yet, so he sat down and waited in the same spot he had earlier that day.

Reflecting on the day's events, his heart filled with anxiety. He thought about his involvement with Marlena and how much trouble it could cause, especially here in Eve. He also flashed back to the look and hug Marlena had given the man she met outside the cafe. He thought that must have been her real boyfriend. He was saddened by the thought that their was no real chance for a woman as accomplished as her to fall deeply in love with a man with his modest background.

His mind shifted to Ricky. He felt sorry for the young boy and he wondered if there was anything he could do for him. Deep down he knew he could help, but realized that in the short amount of time he was going to be in Eve there was only so much he could do. He made a pact with himself to help less fortunate youth whenever he could. As a start, he would somehow find a way to help Ricky work his way out of the cage of his own destiny.

Reflecting on his feelings for Marlena, Adam felt a twinge of guilt. He thought about Teri and every other single sister he knew who was having trouble finding a decent man to settle down with. He wondered if what he was doing was the right thing.

"Hi, handsome. Waiting for someone?" Marlena said playfully.

Her voice was as sweet as cotton candy, and Adam's thoughts were quickly pushed into the back of his mind. He looked up at her and smiled. When his eyes met hers, all of the magic they shared instantly took effect. The only thing that mattered was
this moment, and they held their gaze.

Adam's mouth began to water. He licked his lips, then lowered his thick eyebrows into a devilish expression. "I could eat you for breakfast, lunch, and dinner."

Marlena was taken aback by Adam's newfound forwardness. "Whew!" she exclaimed as her jaw dropped. She put her hand to her cheek.

"I'm sorry," he said. "I am so sorry. I meant no offense. Maybe that was a little too forward. Please forgive me."

They stepped aside as another teacher walked out of the building and passed where they were standing. When the other teacher was far enough away, Marlena explained, "It's okay. I'm not offended in the least. I was just a little surprised. I didn't know you had that kind of aggression in you. Actually, it was kind of nice. Maybe one day you'll actually have an opportunity to have me as your entire day's nourishment. Better not eat for a while, though." As she spoke, her eyes became as devilish as his. This time, Adam was the shocked one. His eyebrows raised in a nervous, anticipatory look. Again their eyes locked and his mouth began to water. He shook his head and suggested, "We had better get out of here. I'm parked in the guest spot around back."

Marlena reached out and grabbed his hand as they walked to his car.

"So, you'll find your way to Sam's place?" she asked.

"Yes, I remember."

An old, navy blue Chevy loaded with a group of Eve's more delinquent citizenry drove past. As the car sped by, one of the passengers stuck his head out and hollered, "Nigger go home!"

Adam and Marlena couldn't make out the man's face because of the Grim Reaper mask he was wearing. Both the mask and the statement were a clear message to Adam that his welcome was quickly wearing thin.

Marlena turned and said, "Ignorance! I can't believe these people are still caught up in blind hate." She looked at Adam. "Are you all right?"

Adam just stood there staring in the direction of the speeding car. He felt despondent and wondered why he was in this place.

"Adam!"

"Yeah, Marlena, I'm fine," he mumbled. "I've just never experienced a town like this before. I feel like I'm in one of those movies about bigotry in the south—like this isn't even real. What am I doing here anyway? You know, sometimes I feel like there is someone up there guiding me along. Putting me in circumstances and situations that test me. Sometimes, I can't really figure out what's going on, what purpose a situation is serving toward my growth, and this is one of those situations. I keep coming back to the question, why am I here? Why now? Why do I feel like I could fall in love with you at the drop of a hat? Why does part of me feel like that is the worst possible thing for me to do right now?"

Marlena could see the sadness in his eyes. She empathized with his hurt and her anger built even more. She took a breath to calm herself. "Adam, don't get yourself all worked up. I think you're probably the sweetest man I've ever met. The ignorance here is just that, blind ignorance. Don't try and make too much sense of it because it could drive you insane. There may be a lesson in this for you. It quite possibly has more to do with how absolutely brilliant and above this you are. This type of bigotry has existed for years. It sometimes seems like it will never go away, but I see otherwise. It is a slow, evolutionary process we may never live to see fully develop. However, there will be a drastic change in attitudes by the time our great-grandchildren walk this planet. It starts now, with our attitude toward today's children."

She looked off into the distance and continued. "We must live in a way that demonstrates brotherhood and humanity, even in the face of hatred. We must show today's children the beauty of our differences, offering an exchange of cultures and ideas. Adam, don't let this steer your gentle spirit down the wrong path—the path of hate and contempt. You know deep down in your heart you are ultimately unchallengeable. No one can touch the beauty of who you really are. It is clear to me who you are and that's why I'm so drawn to you."

Adam just stood quietly, staring in the direction that the bigot's car went. Finally he turned to Marlena and solemnly said, "Marlena, thank you for all your kind words, but I'm sorry. I think this town sucks and I'm going to get out of here as fast as humanly possible. I don't think my purpose in life is to change the minds of all the little children being raised by bigots. I don't like this situation, and nothing personal, but I want out. This is getting far too complicated. Now if you don't mind, we had better go."

Marlena pursed her lips in frustration, then wiped the single tear running down her cheek. The two got into Adam's car and drove away. During the trip home not more than three words were spoken between them. There was only two feet between them, yet they were worlds apart.

14.

Adam pulled his car in front of the Thompson home and came to a stop. He turned towards Marlena. "Marlena, I really am sorry, but I'm having trouble dealing with the situation in this town. Please don't think this is in any way directed towards you."

"Adam," Marlena interrupted, "please, I understand. You don't have to explain your anger to me. I think I know where it comes from. I guess I thought we shared similar feelings for each other."

"What do you mean?"

"Well, how do I put this, Adam? It didn't take long to see I could fall in love with you. Shortly thereafter, I realized I had. The way the world views you and what we share will never change the way I feel for you. There is nothing outside of us that could taint the beauty I see in you. I feel a warm glow every time I think of you and the prospect of spending time with you. Your skin color or race play no part in what I feel."

She looked into his eyes. "The only anger I feel is when people try to impose their fear and ignorance on us. Ultimately it is their pain they are trying to release and that doesn't have much to do with us at all. They have to live with that. The only difference between us is that you're a man and I'm a woman. I love the man you are. I guess I assumed you felt the same. Not so much the love, but the part of you that does love. The part that knows, if we do in fact belong together, there is nothing that is a threat to our happiness."

Adam took a deep breath and sat silently for a moment as Marlena stared out the window.

After a moment, she turned to him and said, "Well, I guess I just gave you a mouthful. I better let you get going."

"Wait! Wait, don't go." Adam paused, trying to find the right words. "Marlena, I do have feelings for you. I'm very affected by this town and the bigotry I experience here. I just feel like I need to back off and gather my thoughts. This is too much for me at one time."

Marlena looked into Adam's eyes and solemnly stated, "I understand." She reached up and ran her hand across his cheek, her disappointment obvious from her slightly pouting lip. No words needed to be spoken. Their love was undeniable. Their future together, however, was anything but certain.

Marlena opened the door and got out of the car. When she closed the door behind her, she waved good-bye. Forcing a smile, she turned and walked away. Adam watched as she moved up the walk into her house. As she closed the door behind her, Adam sped off. He tried not to think about his current circumstances, especially the feelings he had for Marlena. Of all of his current misfortunes, the dilemma over how to handle his affection for Marlena was the most troubling.

He tried to focus on his aircraft and getting it airborne again. He also tried thinking of the anticipated meeting with Sam, the man who had pulled him from his plane after the crash. His thoughts just kept coming back to her—the way she moved, the way her eyes glimmered when she looked at him, the softness of her lips, and the warm electricity he felt every time she was near. The way he felt about her didn't make any sense to him. He barely knew her. She was from a different culture with a completely different view of the world. To try and be with her would only cause trouble, he thought. Maybe the best thing was to just get out of town as soon as possible and try to forget about her.

In the meantime, he could try and associate with "his people." Maybe Teri—she was certainly attractive enough to spend time with. He tried to think of a way to find someone else he could stay with while he was here. Maybe he would find someone at the black baptist church he was to visit on Sunday.

As he drew closer to the turnoff to Sam's property, he began to focus more on what he would say. Obviously, he was eternally grateful for everything Sam had done that fateful evening of his crash. He wondered how he could repay him for his courageous deed. He drove up the dirt road leading to Sam's house. Approximately a quarter mile and off to the right, he could see his Malibu sitting among the trees. He continued on until he came to another group of trees. He could see Sam's modest residence just past the small, wooded area.

He pulled up next to the house. As soon as he shut off his motor, an old man of about sixty-five came walking out the front door. It looked like it could be a nineteenth-century cabin. The man was about six feet tall. He had an angular, craggy face. He looked like an old cowboy with a well-aged swagger.

"Well now, I see you are up and at it. How are you feeling, young man?" Sam said like a long-lost relative as he moved towards Adam.

"Well, I've been better, but under the circumstances I feel pretty good."

Sam shook his hand, and they looked at each other and smiled. Sam reached down with his other hand and wrapped it around Adam's as they continued their warm handshake. The affection this old fellow seemingly had for him seemed a little odd.

Sam looked into Adam's eyes. "It's good to see you doing well, son. I'm glad that you came by."

Adam, feeling the same emotion and gratitude that had first inspired him to come and see Sam, looked at him and smiled. "I had to come over and thank you for pulling me from my plane and getting me some help. I don't know how long I would have been out here if you hadn't come along."

Adam's eyes began to mist up. He looked away, as men sometimes do, to cover the depth of his feeling. He wiped his eyes to insure the tears would not make their way down his cheek, implying he was soft. He looked back at Sam, having regained his composure.

"How did you know I was there? Did you see me coming down?" Adam asked.

Sam smiled and looked at the ground in contemplation. "Well," he said, "It really was just dumb luck, I guess. It was storming that night and I heard the thunder just going like crazy. I heard something sound like it hit the side of the house, so I went to check it out. When I got outside, it seemed like it must've just been a tree limb or something. There was no apparent damage. So there I was, just standing on the porch looking out at the storm. When all of a sudden I happened to glance off through those trees and saw what I thought was a light flashing. It kinda threw me for a loop. I really hadn't seen lights like that since the war. I thought to myself, those kinda look like airplane lights. So, not wasting any time, I took off running towards the lights to make sure no one was hurt, and there you were."

"Well, I'm awfully glad you went to the trouble to check it out."

"Well, youngster, dragging you out of that plane was probably just as important for me and it was for you," Sam added in a somber but grateful tone.

"What do you mean by that, Sam?"

Sam scratched his head, then stroked his cheeks with his hand. "Hmm. Why don't we go have a cold one? You know, I'm not one for socializing and drinking these days but I think the old, town pub is still serving a pretty decent pull of beer. If you're interested, it's on me."

Adam insisted he pick up the tab. After all, it was Sam that pulled him from the plane.

"Before you go and start feeling indebted to me for any good deeds, you have to let me explain some things. Okay?"

Adam smiled and nodded. Sam went in the house to grab his things and the two men got into Adam's car and drove off.

15.

Adam and Sam entered the run-down tavern that sat at the edge of town. The room was smoke-filled and they could hear the sound of pool balls crashing into each other on the pool table near the back. The bar was loud with honky-tonk blaring from the old jukebox. With the sound of the door closing behind them, summoning their entrance into this dreadful den, all movement seemed to stop. The three men at the pool table looked over in astonishment. The bartender looked at them, but never stopped wiping down the glasses he was working on. There were two women seated at a table with a group of men, their playful flirtatious laughter cut short. Sam, in his exuberance to fill Adam in, had forgotten where he was.

Sam recognized some of the faces from poking about town, but these weren't people he held in high regard. To Sam, they were people whom life had passed over and forgotten to grace with compassion and peace. To these people he was just "old Sam," the eccentric hermit who lived in the house just outside of town.

Sam and Adam looked around at their faces. Adam grabbed Sam by the arm and motioned him toward the door. Sam, however, had a different agenda. He pulled his arm away. "This country belongs as much to you and me as it does to anyone else. I almost died overseas defendin' the liberties of everyone here. I'll be damned if I can't drink a beer with a friend where I want to." Although Sam was speaking to Adam, it was clear the statement was aimed at anyone who was close enough to hear.

The two men worked their way over to an empty booth and sat down. The noise in the tavern was slowly working its way back to the boisterous level it was at before they entered. Still a bit anxious, Adam settled into his seat and looked over at Sam and smiled. Sam smiled back and the two men began laughing, as if they shared a secret no one else in the room knew.

"Oh, boy," Adam sighed. "Sam, I think these have been the strangest two days of my life. It is hard for me to believe this whole situation. I crashed my plane. I'm not in the town I am supposed to be in—changing the course my life. Instead, I'm here, in a place that seems to hate my very presence more than anything. I called home to tell my girlfriend my condition and some guy answers the phone. I bet they were both still lying in bed together. Boy, that still burns me up. I have three cracked ribs, a mild concussion, and it looks like I'll be stuck here until I can get someone down here to fix my airplane. To top it all off, I think I'm falling in love with someone that I shouldn't."

They just sat there for a moment while Sam searched for the right words. Adam shook his head in disgusted amazement at his situation.

Adam looked around the bar and pondered out loud, "I wonder how many people in this place would like to see me dead? How many wish my plane had just crashed into the ground and gone up in flames?"

Adam looked at Sam, scrunched his eyebrows, and asked, "Why'd you do it Sam? Why did you pull me out and drag me so far in a storm? What possessed you?"

"We'll get to that, youngster," Sam answered. "What'll ya have to drink? Beer?"

Adam, a little amused by the response, smiled and nodded. "Yeah, beer is fine."

Sam got up and walked over to the bar. He looked at the bartender, who appeared to be ignoring him. "The service is a little slow around here. My friend and I would like to have a couple of beers. Stroh's if you've got it."

The bartender, who was standing at the end of the bar talking to a couple of the local heavies, didn't flinch. It was as if Sam didn't even exist. Sam's short temper began to show itself in his facial expression.

One of the men had long stringy black hair covered with a yellow, *Diesel Power* cap. He twirled the bottom of his fu-manchu mustache with his fingers and looked up at Sam with a cold, black gaze, "You know, old man, we don't much like socializing or drinking with niggers or with crazy old coots who hang around niggers."

The three men started laughing. The tension was building in Sam's face as he looked at them. "Okay, I guess I misunderstood. I'll just use your restroom and go somewhere else then. Could you direct me to it?"

The bartender pointed behind his two acquaintances and said, "Right around that corner, old man, and make it quick."

Sam turned and headed towards the restroom. He walked behind where the two men were sitting. They were still giggling about their rude comments. He turned and quickly grabbed his chief tormentor by the throat. He pulled him up from his bar stool and before anyone could react, Sam had a grip around the man's throat that could break his neck if he twisted it enough.

"Now then," Sam exclaimed, "my friend and I just thought we would come into your nice, friendly establishment and quench our thirst while we caught up on old times. We didn't expect there to be any trouble. You know, the last time I held a man like this was in Sicily, 1944. He was a Nazi fellow, I snuck up on him outside an apartment building. One short jerk and he fell to the ground like a bag of rocks. I never did find out what became of that poor fellow but, like you, he was in the wrong place at the wrong time."

Sam tightened his grip around the unfortunate man's neck and he let out a groan. As he held the man by the neck, Sam politely asked, "My friend over there, Adam, and I are awfully thirsty. Do you think you could arrange for a couple of beers for us?"

Gasping for air, the man looked up at the bartender, who was watching with apprehension. The bartender nodded. As the bartender began to pour the brews, Sam noticed the attention of the room was again focused on him.

Adam was up and walking toward Sam to assist him. "Is everything all right Sam?"

Sam assured him all was well and told him he would be right over with the drinks. Adam, a bit confused, went back and sat down at the table.

Sam soon rejoined Adam at the table. He looked at him and cheerfully said, "Hell, don't worry, son. I've dealt with worse than them. They just need to be reeducated a bit. They don't understand that a man's a man, it don't matter how he may look. We're all the same. Except I guess some of us are more brave than others."

Adam just sat there with a blank look on his face. He wondered what else could possibly happen to him in this town. He wondered if he would ever get back on track, or if he just needed to get out of town and come back later after all of the repairs on his plane had been completed. It had begun to feel like a very reasonable alternative.

As he worked through his alternatives, his mood began to lighten. He tried to focus on Sam, who was rambling on about his intolerance of ignorant people and how he should be respected more for putting his life on the line against the Nazis.

Adam looked over at Sam just as he was completing one of his rambling statements.

He gave him a half-hearted smile and nodded, feigning approval of his sentiments. It wasn't that he didn't agree, it's just that he wasn't paying attention. He didn't want to offend Sam by telling him he wasn't listening.

"Sam, thanks again. I don't know where I would be if you hadn't pulled me out of that plane when you did. Maybe one of these people would have," he said, motioning toward the locals. "God only knows where I'd be now if one of them had pulled me out instead." Adam shook his head at the thought. "That could've been a fate worse than death."

Sam lowered his head and stared at his beer for a moment. He had a little smirk on his face. "Well, don't go feeling indebted to me for pulling you out of your circumstance. I had to do it."

"Had to? You said that before. Just what do you mean, Sam?"

"Yep, as a matter of fact I've been waiting for you to fall out of the sky for the better part of fifty years now."

"What?" Adam exclaimed. "Sam, are you okay? You're freakin' me out, old man."

Sam chuckled. "Before you go and call me crazy, youngster, let me explain. I have been indebted to the universe since the war—the big one, you know. I was in Europe during my tour. Fresh out of boot camp, young and full of vim, achin' for the chance to give those Nazis some hell. My company got pinned down and was darn near wiped out when we heard the order to pull back and retreat. We started running like all get-up. There were bullets whizzin' by—bombs exploding all around us. We were running for our lives with the Nazis bearing down hard. Our numbers were dwindlin'. It reached a point where I didn't even know where I was running to. I was just running to get away from those Nazis. I reached a clearing and paused for a minute. The gunfire seemed to be in the distance, so I started trotting across a clearing. Then, boom! A mortar shell exploded no more than fifty feet away and gunfire was whizzin' right by my head again. I could see a fighter plane headed in my direction. I thought to myself, this is it. I'm going to die right here in this field."

Adam leaned forward, intrigued.

"When the fighter flew over me, he was low enough I could see he was one of ours. I jumped behind some boulders to my left and laid there for a moment. As I looked back towards the forest, I could see the Nazis comin' right at me. I raised my rifle and started firing at 'em. There was no way I could beat 'em, but I wasn't going down like a coward. Just then the fighter made a second pass, heading directly towards the Germans and boom, rat-a-tat-tat. He dropped a load on a bunch of 'em, sprayin' 'em with gunfire. It inspired me."

Adam, who was now on the edge of his seat listening to old Sam's tale, nodded.

"I raised up and started firing like there was no tomorrow, which at that point I didn't feel there was gonna be. The fighter made one more pass and things got real quiet. Then, I saw him coming down real slow. I thought he had been shot down or something. He came closer and closer until he finally flared his wings and put down as soft as a bird, no more than a hundred feet from me. I didn't know if he was having technical problems or what. So I looked over at him, then pointed my rifle at the Germans to give him some cover. I heard him give it gas and the plane spun around with its nose towards the Nazis. Then, the damnedest thing, he pops open the hatch and jumps out. He motioned for me to come, but I couldn't because I had a big gash running up my thigh. Besides, I was in shock. That pilot was a colored. I didn't even know they let coloreds fly back then. I'd never heard of such a thing.

"The gunfire from the Germans was picking up and we could see them coming out of the trees. The pilot had made his way over to me and drug me back to his P-40. He got me into the back of the cockpit, jumped in, and started it up. A mortar shell exploded close by. Boy, I was scared to death and totally amazed at the same time. Then a bullet found its way through the top of the canopy. He hit his guns and the soldiers coming out of the trees started dropping like flies. He gunned his engine and we started rolling towards them at full speed, guns a-blazin'. We took off and just nicked a tree branch. We got outta there just barely scratched. It was the most amazing day in all of my seventy-ought years. When the pilot was putting me into the fighter, he dropped this medallion in my lap."

Sam pulled the medallion out of his pocket and showed it to Adam. Adam was completely silent, looking at the impressive piece of old jewelry. Sam seemed a bit melancholy as he worked it around in his hands.

"I went by his barracks—Lieutenant Jefferson was his name—to try and thank him and return his medallion. When I did find his barracks, they told me he had been shot down and killed on a mission a couple days after we had returned. I've been haunted by that day ever since. Wishing, hoping, praying that someday I could repay that fine young soldier. I feel like pulling you out sort of gave me a chance at redemption. When I saw you were colored, I knew it was God giving me a shot at repaying some of the good that has made it possible for me to be walking around today."

He looked into Adam's eyes.

"Son, my biggest feeling right now is gratefulness. I'm glad I could help you in your time of need. You don't have to thank me anymore. Thank you for going through what you did to give me a chance to bring closure to a part of my life. I guess Lieutenant Jefferson would've liked for you to have this."

He reached over and handed Adam the medallion. Adam brought it closer to get a better look. After inspecting it he said,

"Wow, this thing is incredible."

Sam's smile said it all. The opportunity to do the good he waited a lifetime for had finally come.

Adam looked up and held out the medallion. "I couldn't possibly take this. It's too valuable. Think of the memories it holds for you."

Sam just shook his head. "Son, er, Adam, I can't continue on unless you accept this gift. If you are so set on thanking me for pulling you out of your airplane, do it by letting me give you this. I truly believe it belongs in your hands now. Besides, it is supposedly a good luck charm. Judging by your circumstances, you could use some. I only wish the lieutenant would've had it with him on his last flight. He might still be alive. " Sam raised his voice, almost in desperation. "Take it. Go on, take it."

The other tavern patrons were turning to see what was going on.

Adam hesitantly nodded as he held his new treasure. He felt honored to have it. He was very aware of the reputation of the first black flyers in World War II, known as the Tuskeegee Airman. Now he had a piece of their history in his hands. Just as incredible were the exploits Sam had just described that had gotten the medallion into his possession.

Sam and Adam finished their conversation and stood up to leave. As they walked across the room, they received looks of disdain from those around them, especially the men Sam had the confrontation with. As they walked out the door, they heard a voice loudly bellow, "Watch your back, old man."

Adam turned and looked at Sam with concern.

Sam just stared straight ahead. "After what I've seen and experienced in my life, those rogues in there don't worry me in the least. They're ignorant and that's not entirely their fault. They're just acting out the way their parents taught them to." Sam's voice had a somber tone, almost prophetic.

The two men's eyes met as they stood on opposite sides of the car. Sam smiled. "There must have been 150 of them Nazis bearing down on me."

Adam smiled back, though somewhat hesitantly.

16.

"Dad, you have to use whatever influence you have in this town. Whatever happened to the ideals you instilled in me growing up? You can't just stand idly by and let this sort of behavior continue. It won't just go away."

"Marlena, I understand how upset you are about what happened to Adam today—"

"No, Dad, me! I am also talking about what happened to me! I was there, remember? What would you do if it had been rape, or some other physical abuse?"

"Austin, she's right," Sara said. "Someone in this town is going to have to make a stand to redefine acceptable behavior. In the past you haven't hesitated to take a stand. It seems you've become tentative about what to do, even to the point of making excuses about why you shouldn't do anything. I don't understand what has completely changed your views."

"If you vipers would just let me finish, maybe you could gain a little understanding. I do agree what happened was wrong—"

"Then do something!" Marlena shouted.

Sara gave her a stern look. "Marlena, if you don't be quiet, we'll never resolve this. Now, shut up! Please."

"Well, thank you." Austin said. "This is not a good time in my life to pick the wrong fights. I am not here to change this little town. I am here to try and put my—our—financial situation back together. If I can't get myself in a position to buy another publication in either the Rockies or the Northwest in the next couple of years, we could end up stuck here for a very long time. Now, as much as I don't like it, sometimes we just have to make sacrifices for a broader, long-term vision."

Adam walked in the front door. Marlena, not really paying attention to the door, didn't notice his entry. "You mean compromise your values and morals so life goes on without a hitch, right?" She said.

As Adam entered the room, all three Thompsons turned to look at him. The expressions on their faces indicated he had just walked in on something he shouldn't have.

Adam looked at them. "Did I come in at a bad time?"

"Adam, we were just discussing the incident you and Marlena were involved in this afternoon in town," Sara said.

"Specifically, how some of us can sit idly by and let these type of things go on without saying anything about how wrong they are," Marlena added sharply.

"Adam, Marlena feels strongly that Austin should use his authority as publisher and chief editor of the local paper to write an editorial condemning the type of behavior the two of you experienced this afternoon."

Adam sat down and thought for a minute. "You know," he said thoughtfully, "I really appreciate everything you have done for me since I got here. You have been more than gracious in your hospitality. If part of your dilemma involves what I will think of you, please don't worry. You are perhaps the most loving people I have ever had the pleasure to know. I think I have a pretty good sense of what motivates you. At least it appears you don't mean anyone any harm. So don't feel like you have to defend me or who I am. Mr. Thompson, please, if any of this brings you grief, don't do it, especially on my account."

"I don't believe this," Marlena said.

"I really feel as if you have already done too much for me," Adam continued. "Mr. Thompson, Mrs. Thompson..."

He looked over at Marlena. The expression on his face showed the love he felt, as well as the hurt of knowing this was a love that would never be. He looked into her eyes and saw her sadness.

"Old Sam offered to let me stay in his spare room until the Malibu's repairs are completed. The work is going to be done right there on his property, so it would be very convenient. I really appreciate everything you've done. The mechanic is due in the morning, so I'll probably go over there then."

The room went silent. Sara and Austin glanced at each other and raised their eyebrows.

Marlena just sat staring into space. Adam's decision to move implied more than convenience. It was a clear symbol to her that either he didn't have the courage or possibly the inclination to continue their relationship.

Adam timidly glanced at Marlena, but she wouldn't look in his direction. Instead, she focused on the Monet hanging on the wall across from where she was sitting. Sara had a clear view of her daughter's face and could see her disappointment. She could also feel Marlena's despair as she watched the tears well up in her eyes.

Sara's voice cracked as she said, "If you all will excuse me, I think I'll retire for the evening. A lot has happened today and I'm feeling drained from it."

She turned and left the living room, climbing the stairs that led to the bedroom.

"Well, I should probably get some rest too." Adam said. He nodded as he acknowledged Marlena and Austin. "Mr. Thompson."

Austin nodded back, bidding him a good night. Adam then turned toward Marlena. "Marlena."

She continued staring at the Monet, a tear rolling down the cheek that was turned from Adam. He couldn't see her expression, nor was he aware of how deeply she was hurt. He paused to take her in for a moment, then turned and went to his room

In an attempt to make amends, Austin moved toward.

Marlena.

"Marlena I know you're disappointed at my—"

"Save it, Dad. Could you just leave me alone? I just want to sit here alone for awhile."

"Well, yes, certainly honey. We'll talk more about this in the morning after everyone has cooled off."

Marlena's only response was a subtle shake of her head.

As he walked into the bedroom, his reception from Sara was chilly at best. She sat propped up against a mound of pillows on the bed reading a book.

"What's that?" he asked in an attempt to strike up a conversation.

She lifted the book up and held the title towards him so he could read it. She didn't say a word. The message was very clear. Austin's decision to not take a moral stand had alienated him from the women in his family—those who meant the most to him. In the past he had done everything in his power to preserve the values he instilled in his daughter. These same values were a big part of why Sara had fallen in love with him in the first place. Now it seemed he was taking the easy way out of an uncomfortable situation and justifying it as being necessary for financial survival.

"Sara, you have to understand my point of view," he said. "If I set off a powder keg in this town, I will lose substantial ad revenues and possibly alienate a big segment of the paper's readership. Who knows if the paper could rebound from that? I've lost one publication and look where that landed me—in this godforsaken place. If I lose another, God only knows where we'll end up!"

Sara calmly put her book down. "Austin, I have been poor with you before. Granted, it was not as convenient as the life we have now, but the ideals we lived by meant more than living in a nice house, traveling, or buying nice things ever will. I don't know how the fear I am seeing in you has gotten so imbedded in your soul, but it's unwarranted. If you honestly believe what truly matters is how Marlena and I feel about you, then I'm telling you, we don't care how you provide for us financially. As far as I'm concerned, the rest of society can just kiss your ass. Anyway, Marlena is independent as it is. The only reason she stays here is her passion to help make a difference. She's paying as much rent as she would anywhere else."

Austin nodded.

"If you make a stand for what you truly believe, we will respect that more than any amount of material success you could provide. Austin, deep down in your heart you know the right thing to do. I just hope you aren't too battered to do it."

Austin was touched by his wife's sentiments and lowered his head. She was right. Deep down he knew what his heart was telling him to do. The question was whether or not he had the courage left to carry it out.

At two o'clock in the morning, the phone rang. Austin looked to see if Sara was awake; she wasn't. Half asleep, he reached for the phone and groggily answered. "Hello?"

There was no response.

Again he said, "Hello," this time a little perturbed.

A gruff voice on the other end of the phone muttered, "Get rid of the nigger, or we will!"

There was a click and the phone went silent. Austin hung up and laid back on his pillow, staring at the ceiling. By this time, Sara was half awake.

"Who was it, Austin?"

"It was no one," he replied. "Just some kids playing on the phone."

17.

Adam rose just before dawn. He had a busy day ahead and didn't want to fall behind schedule. He wanted to be packed and gone from the Thompsons' home before anyone was awake, to avoid having to further explain his leaving.

With everything packed into his duffel bags, Adam quietly made his way downstairs. He could see the flaming orange sunrise as he passed the big picture window in the dining room. He paused to take it in.

"Magnificent, isn't it!" Sara commented.

Adam was startled as he whirled around to see Sara leaning against the wall, sipping her morning brew. She raised her coffee mug, inviting him to join her.

"Shall I pour you a cup?"

"No, I really must be going," Adam replied.

Sara, unaffected by his obvious discomfort, coolly looked up at him. "Surely your mechanic isn't due at the crack of dawn, is he?"

Adam sensed the playfulness mixed with her sarcasm and relaxed. "Well, no, he isn't due for a couple of hours. I was just trying to get an early start."

He followed her into the kitchen and she began pouring him a cup of the fresh coffee.

"Black?" she queried.

"Cream and sugar," he replied.

She gestured for him to join her at the kitchen table. As the two sat down, they looked at each other and simultaneously let out a sigh. They mirrored each other's nervous actions, circling their fingers around the lips of their mugs.

"Well, it's been quite a trip," Adam said, searching for a way to initiate conversation.

"Yes, indeed. I can imagine this being one of your more challenging weeks. Crashing your plane, er, aircraft and all. You know, Adam, you're welcome to stay here as long as you like."

"Yes, Mrs. Thompson, I know, and I truly appreciate all you've done, but right now I think it would be easier for all of us if I just stayed with Sam."

"I understand, Adam. You don't have to explain. However, I would like to ask you a question."

There was a moment of awkwardness as they sat peering into their half empty mugs.

"Okay, ask away."

"Do you love her?"

"What!"

"Adam, if you truly—"

"Wait a minute, Mrs. Thompson. I believe you mean well, but this is going too far. I am here because of circumstances beyond my control, and as soon as I get things back on track, I'll be gone. As wonderful as Marlena is, this is not the place to be falling in love. At least not with someone who could get me killed."

Sara simply raised her eyebrows and calmly asked, "Was that a yes or a no?"

"I don't believe this," he murmured. He grabbed his bag and hastily headed for the front door. "I really appreciated the hospitality, Mrs. Thompson. I don't know how I'll ever repay your kindness and generosity. Now, if you will excuse me, I'd better be going." He reached to open the door.

"Adam," Sara called out.

He turned and looked at her as she patted the middle of her chest with her hand.

"Trust your heart," she said.

Adam paused for a moment with his lips pursed tightly together. He turned back toward the door and walked out, closing it behind him.

Sara walked over to the window and saw him pause again on the porch. As he began to walk away, she whispered, "And listen to what it says."

18.

A police car pulled into the driveway behind the blue rental car Adam was driving. The sheriff and his deputy calmly exited their vehicle and walked over to Adam. "Good morning, Mr. Freeman. Getting an early start today, I see."

"Morning. Yeah, I'm supposed to meet my mechanic this morning to try and get my aircraft airborne again."

Sara, noticing the arrival of the two officers, walked out onto the front porch. "Good morning, Sheriff Phillips. What brings you to our humble home this early in the day?"

"Well, Mrs. Thompson, we received a tip this morning that something was amiss over at old Sam's place. When we arrived we found Sam dead. His throat had been cut with a broken beer bottle."

"Oh my God!" Sara gasped.

Adam shook his head in disbelief and he silently stared at the ground. The deputy had subtly positioned himself next to Adam as the sheriff continued. "We've talked to a few people who were at the bar last night. It seems that Adam, here, was the last one seen with Sam. Furthermore, we were able to pull a set of prints off the broken glass that was used as the murder weapon. The prints matched those we took from Mr. Freeman's airplane."

Sara and Adam looked at each other, sensing what was happening.

Sara looked at Sheriff Phillips and nervously asked, "So, Sheriff, just what are you getting at?"

The sheriff turned to his deputy and motioned to him with a nod of his head. Deputy Lake grabbed Adam by his wrist, as Sheriff Phillips said, "Mr. Freeman, you are under arrest for the murder of Sam Stinson. You have the right…"

Sara began screaming as she ran back into the house. "Austin, Austin come here quickly. Austin!"

As Adam was being pushed into the police car, he could see the Thompsons' porch and Marlena, Sara, and Austin walking quickly toward him. The door to the car shut just as they got close enough to talk to him.

Austin leaned down and spoke through the glass, "Adam, Adam, we'll meet you down at the station. We're going to straighten this whole thing out."

Sara and Marlena stepped back as the sheriff's car backed out onto the road, turned, and sped off.

As Adam was put through the normal procedures, finger prints, mug shots, etc…he noticed the musty smell of cigarettes permeate the room. He looked to his left and noticed the confederate flag hanging. It covered almost one-third of the wall.

It had been a long time since Adam felt as if his destiny was out of his own control. His power to make his life whatever he wished had been completely striped away. His powerlessness unnerved him and he felt on the verge of a collapse. As Adam and the deputy entered the cell block, the deputy closed the door behind them. The light was dimmer now as they walked down the short corridor. Adam could see only one other person occupying a cell.

As they walked by the prisoner's quarters, Adam looked in at the old, black man sitting on the bench. He seemed broken and the sadness in his eyes told of generations of pain. The man looked back at Adam and shook his head. Adam wasn't sure he understood the gesture.

Deputy Lake forcefully grabbed Adam's arm and shoved him into his jail cell. When he slammed the door, he peered in at Adam and sneered, "You are one troublesome nigger. We don't like smart-ass niggers in this town, boy. We always find a way to get rid of people like you who think they are better than the decent people of this town. Why'd you do it?"

Adam was startled by the question and could only manage to respond, "Do what?"

"Why did you kill old Sam? That must've been some argument you guys had in front of the tavern." Deputy Lake smirked. "Boy, you're going to love prison. That is, if you live long enough to see it."

Adam sunk into his cot and placed his head in his hands and quietly wept.

"Why? Why, why, why am I here? What did I do to deserve this shit? My life is over. It would've been easier to have been killed by the impact of the crash. Maybe I was and this is hell," he murmured softly to himself as he laid back on the cot, staring at the dark walls.

He closed his eyes and drifted off to sleep. In his dream he was walking through lush woods with Marlena close behind. She wore the floral print dress she had on the first time he saw her. As they walked along, the trail began to ascend an enormous mountain. It started raining as they continued to climb higher and higher. Finally, they reached a clearing. They were unaware of the danger of exposure they faced from being out so long in the pouring rain. The thunder and lightning began as they looked longingly into each other's eyes. They embraced and started to kiss passionately. They were drenched, yet they were oblivious to anything but the warmth they felt in each other's arms.

Adam woke up with a start, not remembering where he was. When the reality of his circumstance set in, he sighed and again closed his eyes.

19.

The creaking sound of the heavy, cellblock door rang through the cell area. Adam woke up as the door slammed closed. He could hear two sets of footsteps walking in his direction. He sat up on the bed and looked toward the cell door.

The sheriff reached the cell first and stuck his key into the lock. As he opened the door he announced, "Son, you have a visitor."

Reverend Jacobson stood in the doorway.

"Jes, you have ten minutes," the sheriff advised.

The reverend kindly thanked him, then gave Adam a warm smile. He shook his head. "You've gotten yourself in a heap of trouble, ain't you, boy?"

"I didn't kill him. Why would I kill Sam?" Adam said defiantly, as he bolted up from the bed. "He pulled me from my plane the night I went down. This doesn't make sense."

The reverend put his hands on Adam's shoulders in an attempt to calm him down. "Son, this sort of thing happens all of the time around here. I'm just glad you're still breathing. The sheriff is a fairly decent man, so if you're telling the truth there's a chance we can get you out of here. Now what happened last night?"

Adam sat back down on the cot and thought for a minute. "Well, basically, Sam and I had gone to this hick tavern on the edge of town. It was set way back off of the main road behind the trees."

"You went to Jake's? Oh my God, boy! What did you go and do a thing like that for?" Jacobson exclaimed.

Not quite knowing how to respond, Adam shrugged. "I didn't know where we were going. It was where Sam suggested going for a beer. He said he hadn't been there for a while."

"Okay. Go on, son."

"When we got there it was taking awhile for anyone to come and take our order, so Sam got perturbed. He walked up to the bar to get us some beers and I saw him getting into it with the bartender and a couple of the guys that were sitting at the bar. When he returned to the table, he had our beers. We talked for awhile and he told me some wild story about how one of the Tuskeegee Airmen saved his life in a battlefield in World War II. He gave me this medallion."

Adam opened the top couple buttons of his shirt and showed the reverend the medallion. "Then I took him home."

Reverend Jacobson rubbed his chin and asked, "That's it? That's the whole story?"

"That's pretty much it, sir."

"Adam, listen to me. You are going to give the sheriff the same information you just gave me. You will also be very cooperative and do whatever he tells you to do."

"Reverend Jacobson, I hate to tell you this, but that deputy is a total asshole. I must've gotten the 'hey, nigger' treatment a half dozen times from him."

The reverend nodded. "Yeah, I know. Clint is bad news. Especially when he gets around others like himself. Their fear spreads like a virus. They could stir up the entire town with their white power crap. You just sit tight, son. We'll get you out of here."

Adam looked at Reverend Jacobson with a glimmer of hope, although it was somewhat jaded. At least it was more than he had a few hours ago.

The sheriff walked back to the cell block and called to Reverend Jacobson that his time was up. When he got to the cell door to let him out, he also motioned for Adam to come with him.

"We want to ask you a few questions, son. Come along with me."

"Just a minute, sheriff. Can I have a few words with you before you take him?" Reverend Jacobson said.

"What is it, Jessie?" the sheriff responded, sounding slightly perturbed.

The reverend motioned Sheriff Phillips to a more private spot. When the two men were on the other side of the cell block, the reverend said, "Sheriff, you know that boy didn't kill Sam. He's got no motive."

"We have eyewitnesses that saw the two men arguing and heard Adam threaten Sam in the parking lot of the tavern. We also have the broken bottle that was used to cut the old man's throat. It has flyboy's fingerprints all over it. That's enough."

"Sheriff, listen to the boy's story and be open minded. This young man was on his way to buy an airport in the Pacific Northwest. What reason would be strong enough to make him want to throw his life away? Killing the man who practically saved his life? Come on, Sheriff, could they have had that severe of a disagreement in such a short period of time? Sheriff Phillips, this whole thing stinks of foul play. I wouldn't be surprised if half of this town goes into an uproar if this situation gets out of hand."

Reverend Jacobson gave Phillips a stern look as he turned and walked out. The sheriff just stood there rubbing his chin. He then went back to get Adam.

"Come with me. I want to ask you a few questions."

Adam followed Sheriff Phillips through the cell block and into a small, dark room with a bright light hanging from the ceiling. The sheriff pulled a chair out and gestured for Adam to sit. Sheriff Phillips walked to the doorway and flipped a light switch for additional lighting. It made the room a little less intimidating.

Deputy Lake entered the room. "Tom, you want me to turn the spotlight back on so we can get down to business?"

Phillips looked over at Adam, who was staring at his nervously twitching hands folded on the table.

"No, Clint," the sheriff responded, "leave them the way they are. As a matter of fact, why don't you take the rest of the night off? I can handle this."

"But, Tom, I collected the evidence. I should be here to interrogate this asshole. I've put a lot of work—"

"Clint, I'll handle the questioning," the sheriff declared in a forceful tone. "You've done a fine job putting this case together. Your report should give me all the information I need." He held out his hand for the file folder filled with papers the deputy was holding.

Lake hesitated for a moment. The sheriff cupped his hand and motioned with his fingers, reaffirming his resolve. Lake handed Sheriff Phillips his report and angrily walked out of the interrogation room.

Phillips opened the file folder and began thumbing through its contents. After briefly skimming the highlights of Lake's report, he turned to Adam. "Now, where should we begin, son?"

Adam shook his head nervously, not knowing how to respond. Phillips kept a steady gaze on Adam, trying to feel him out. As he observed Adam, he looked puzzled. The reverend's plea seemed to be sinking into his psyche. Although one might think he was a hard-assed bigot, like so many others in Eve, the sheriff had a deep sense of fair play and justice.

It was his honesty and intent to uphold the law that had originally gotten him elected sheriff of Eve. Along the way he had succumbed to peer pressure and found himself turning his head on some racially motivated transgressions, but none had been as vindictive as this.

Examples of what had gone unprosecuted and relatively uninvestigated by his office were the defacing of the black Baptist church, charges against town hall because of their discriminatory hiring practices, and even the burning of the church-sponsored activity center for underprivileged minorities. At the time, he rationalized it as just the way things were. If he made too much of an issue of it, he was afraid someone would start paying more attention to his affinity for Kentucky whiskey. In any case, the subtle injustices against the town's minority population went unchecked.

This case, however, seemed to strike a chord with Phillips' sense of morality. Maybe this was the line that needed to be drawn to bring a real sense of justice to this town.

He noticed Adam's slumped posture and asked, "Son, tell me about last night." There was compassion in his voice that seemed to say he was not assuming Adam's guilt.

Adam took a deep breath and began telling his version of what had happened the previous night. He spoke of the experience Sam shared with him of being rescued from the battlefield in World War II.

The sheriff listened intently to every detail, as well as to the inflection in Adam's voice. After Adam finished, the sheriff paused for a moment, pondering his course of action.

"Well, son, that all sounds pretty interesting. What I need to do is check on some of the facts you've given me. I'll let you know sometime tomorrow how we are progressing."

He escorted Adam out of the interrogation room, down the cell block corridor, and into the dark cell Adam now called home. As he closed the door behind Adam, he said, "There is a bit of good news. There is a man in town, says he is an aircraft mechanic. Clint showed him to your plane and I think he started working on it today. He said he'll try and contact you when he has a better feel for exactly what needs to be done."

What Sheriff Phillips neglected to tell Adam was that state law prohibited holding a suspect longer than thirty-six hours without sufficient evidence to file charges. That only left Sheriff Phillips twenty-four hours. Although Deputy Lake had presented him with a reasonable amount of evidence to suggest Adam's guilt, the sheriff had at least some doubt about a possible motive.

He also knew this case went far beyond any legal interpretations necessary to convict. If Adam was put on trial in Eve for the murder of a white man, he would surely be found guilty. The jurors would certainly consist of people who would take pleasure in seeing a black man, especially one as accomplished as Adam, be torn down and sent to death row.

For the first time in his life, Sheriff Phillips had to face himself, both as a law enforcement official and a man. He knew if he took a stand in favor of Adam and released him in spite of the evidence, the outrage of certain segments of the community would be on him. It would mean risking his position as town sheriff, which he had held for more than ten years.

Putting Adam away would be easy enough and would win him favor with the majority of Eve's voting population. It would pretty much secure his position there until he decided to retire. He thought to himself, what would I do if they replaced me as a result of something like this? He couldn't continue to live in Eve as a functioning member of the community if he set Adam free. He would be viewed as a traitor, a "nigger lover," and any number of other things, all of which would severely impact his quality of life. He decided to investigate further to see if there was anything Deputy Lake might have overlooked—anything that would be compelling enough to resolve his dilemma. He wished there was an easy way out.

He returned to his desk and plopped down into the chair. He was showing signs of fatigue, both mental and physical, from the events of the last eighteen hours. Reaching into the top drawer of his desk, he pulled out a small, brown paper bag. He unscrewed the top of the bottle hidden inside, put it to his lips, and took a long drink of the elixir.

He sighed as he screwed the top back on and slid the bag back into the desk drawer. He looked toward the ceiling in a silent plea to God. A few moments passed and he looked back down at Deputy Lake's report. He gave it a look like he expected it to speak to him. It was as if the document we're alive and would offer him a way to get out of this mess.

He opened the report and began examining its contents, only this time he paid closer attention to details. It seemed as if he we're just reviewing things he already knew. As he read on, he became more discouraged. There were no new facts that would lead him to believe anyone other than Adam could possibly have murdered Sam.

He reached the end of the report and sank back down into his seat. The report had been carefully put together and there appeared to be nothing that would clearly indicate Adam's innocence. As much as he was moved by Reverend Jacobson's theory about Adam's innocence, there was nothing concrete to back it up.

He began running the day's events through his mind. First, the call he received from Lake informing him there was something up at old Sam's place. He thought about seeing Sam lying on the floor with his throat cut when he arrived. It was a gruesome scene. There were traces of bloody footprints that matched the shoes Sam was wearing the night he was killed.

Then, he realized there was a glaring omission from Lake's report. The photos—where were the photos? He quickly opened the report and flipped frantically through the pages to see if he had overlooked them. They weren't there. He slid back into his chair and he tentatively looked around the office trying to locate the pictures of the crime scene he and Lake had taken when they examined it. He got up and began searching.

First he went to the closet where the camera was stored. It was hanging up on its usual hook. Lake must not have developed the pictures yet. He opened the back of the camera to retrieve the film and found the camera empty. One of the rules handed down from all previous sheriffs was that the crime scene camera was to always remain loaded with film and backup batteries in case something came up. Perhaps Lake had left the undeveloped film in the crime scene lab, where they developed the pictures.

He walked over to the door into the tiny lab. Someone visiting the jail might assume it was nothing more than a closet and, in fact, that's what it had started out as. Phillips had converted it in his first year as Eve's sheriff. He had learned how to develop film when he was in college at a small, northern Louisiana school. He thought the sheriff's office would be more effective if they could develop their own shots. It enabled them to quickly document a crime scene and to analyze the images at length with the magnification equipment they had.

He entered the lab and looked around for the photographs. When he didn't see them, he tried to locate the undeveloped roll of film. He thoroughly searched every nook and cranny, under stacks of papers, and on the floor. Neither the photos nor the undeveloped roll were anywhere to be found. He walked out of the lab and over to Lake's desk and frantically went through the drawers. Again, he found nothing. His concern was increasing. This could play right into Reverend Jacobson's belief and, if nothing could be proven, the situation could become volatile on both sides.

He picked up the telephone and called the second deputy. "Hello, Lance. I need you to come down here and watch a prisoner. Are you available?"

"Yeah, sure, Sheriff."

"Good. Try and get here as soon as you can. I have something pressing to attend to. "

20.

The second deputy pulled up to the sheriff's office and hastily got out of his unmarked vehicle. Sheriff Phillips met him on the stairway outside.

"Lance, thanks for coming. I have to leave right now, so I don't have time to explain. I'll talk to you when I return."

The sheriff wasn't sure about Lance's allegiance, so he didn't risk giving him the entire scenario. If it got out that he was actually looking further into this case because he had doubts about the evidence, it could mean trouble, both for him and Adam.

Phillips got into his car and headed for old Sam's place to see what he could dig up. His heart was pounding as he went through all the possibilities in his mind. Not just about what he would or wouldn't find, but also what his choices would be once he knew exactly what was going on. Somewhere deep inside he felt the reverend was right. He pondered what would become of his life once he freed Adam. Doubts began to creep back into his mind. Could he just go with what he already had? He could stop digging right now and have enough for a conviction. He pulled over to the side of the road to let the thoughts settle. He decided to make a stop at the tavern first, to get a feel for the general sentiment there.

When he arrived at the tavern, he noticed there were several cars in the parking lot. It was a typical, bustling Saturday evening and all the locals were out. He got out of his car and walked toward the entrance. Some of the tavern patrons greeted him as they were leaving.

"Hi, Sheriff Phillips," they said as they staggered toward their cars.

Sheriff Phillips entered the tavern, immediately struck by the noise. The jukebox was blaring. That, combined with the poor sound quality, produced a horrible noise that made the music unbearable to anyone not yet numbed by bourbon. He walked over to the bar, where the bartender was busy making cocktails. The bartender immediately acknowledged the sheriff and told him he would be right over. Phillips waited patiently as he scoped out the room.

"Good evenin', Sheriff. We don't see you much around here. What can I do for you? Whiskey?"

Sheriff Phillips raised his eyebrows. He was taken off guard by the offer, since he was in uniform and obviously still on duty.

"No, Jake. I'm trying to dig up some facts about the murder the other night. I noticed in the report that Clint had questioned you."

"Yeah. I told him what I saw, which wasn't much. I served old Sam a couple beers, then later we saw him and that nigger he was with arguing over there at the booth."

He motioned in the direction of where Adam and Sam had been sitting the night of

Sam's demise. "After that, I couldn't tell you much. I saw them leave together. I heard some people say they saw 'em wrestling a bit in the parking lot, and that's all I know."

Phillips quizzically rubbed his chin as Adam's version of the story ran through his mind. Jake hadn't mentioned anything about the harsh words between Sam and the men at the bar that Adam was unable to identify. There was nothing in Clint's report about a scuffle at the bar, either. There appeared to be two stories surfacing.

"Who was at the bar that night, Jake?"

"Well, Sheriff, it was a busy night. I can't say I really remember everyone at the bar that night," Jake responded coolly.

Phillips wasn't satisfied. "Think, Jake. Was there anyone at the bar you were talking with? Maybe someone that was hanging out and shootin' the breeze with you for awhile."

A few beads of sweat had formed on Jake's forehead. He nervously rubbed his chin and shook his head. "No, I can't say there was, Sheriff. Now if that's all, I got to get back to work."

Phillips glared at Jake. He didn't believe Jake and Jake sensed it.

"Yeah, I think I got all the information I need. Thanks for your trouble, Jake," he said, acting satisfied. "Oh, Jake, one more thing."

Jake turned around, warily. "Yes, Sheriff?" he answered meekly.

"I've changed my mind. I'll take a whiskey. Straight and chase it with some water."

Jake appeared relieved as he let out a subtle sigh. "Coming right up, Sheriff," he said smilling.

Sheriff Phillips downed the shot of whiskey, took a sip of water, and got up from his seat. He waved at Jake and thanked him for his cooperation. As he walked out of the tavern, he knew something was definitely amiss. There were obviously things going on in this case that were beneath the surface. Clint's report seemed to be missing some critical facts, and the only way to get to the truth was to retrace the investigation himself. He decided to start by going back to old Sam's place to see what would turn up.

21.

The patrol car pulled up the long drive, bordered on both sides by huge maple trees. About a quarter mile up the drive the sheriff steered the car right rather than left, which would have taken him to Sam's house. Instead he went in the direction of Adam's aircraft. About three quarters of a mile off the road the terrain became too rugged to drive through, so he stopped the car and turned off the lights. Reaching over, he grabbed his flashlight and got out of the car.

He could see the airplane's paint gleaming in the moonlight. How could a negro afford such a beautiful piece of machinery, he thought as he approached the Malibu. When he got closer, he noticed the airplane's cowling had been removed. He suspected it had been taken off by the mechanic who had arrived earlier that day. Flashing his light into the open cowling, he curiously scanned the airplane's impressive engine. As he moved to the side of plane with the cabin door, he noticed there were a lot of footprints on the ground next to the door. At first he thought nothing of it, but upon closer examination, he noticed there were four or five different sets of prints.

Adam's and Sam's footprints were deeply set into the ground, the mud they sank into the stormy night of Adam's crash was now hardened. It made their footprints easily distinguishable from the rest. He and Clint had been there briefly when they were gathering evidence earlier. He recognized his own footprints. That left Clint and the mechanic. He briskly walked back to the open cowling and flashed his light on the ground where he thought the mechanic would have been working. He studied the prints and went quickly back to the cabin door. Again, he flashed his light on the ground. He found the match to the prints by the cowling. These must have been the mechanic's. There were still three sets of footprints unaccounted for. He knew one had to be Lake's. That still left two. He thought for a moment. Why two extra sets of prints? He mentally filed it away and moved on.

He reached up and pulled the latch on the cabin door. After a few tugs, it swung open. He shined his light into the cockpit, making note of anything that appeared unusual. Two of the dials on the instrument panel were missing. Again, he thought the mechanic must have taken them. Aside from that, everything seemed to be in order. He turned around and flashed the light into the plush-looking cabin. It had dark gray, leather seats. The seats towards the rear of the plane faced forward. The seats closer to the cockpit faced the seats in the back. It looked like a limousine. It seemed as if someone had rummaged through the stowing compartment behind the rear seats, because it was pulled out. The sheriff hung his flashlight from the ceiling, so he could dust for prints.

He followed the standard procedure and collected what he could. When he was finished, he thought it would be a good idea to take another look around Sam's place to see what he could find there.

As he got out of the airplane, he looked it over once more. Walking back toward his patrol car, he began running all of the possibilities through his mind regarding who else might have been there. At this point he was beginning to care less about the fallout and more about getting to the truth of the matter. He felt the surge that originally got him hooked on law enforcement. He was pursuing justice for the first time in years. Upholding that justice became his mission, rather than supporting the status quo. As he approached his vehicle, he looked off into the distance toward old Sam's house.

He slowed down when he noticed a light on inside the house. He was still quite a distance away, and was unable to see what exactly was going on, but he knew there weren't any lights on when he arrived. Since Sam was dead, there should be no one in there. He clicked off his flashlight and walked to the patrol car. He got in and turned the ignition switch. When the car started, he was careful not to gun the gas pedal and make a lot of noise. Sheriff Phillips backed around, all the while keeping his sights set on Sam's house. He was nearly three quarters of a mile off, so the light was a faint, tiny fleck on the horizon, nestled in the darkness of the trees. He shifted into drive and slowly crept in the direction of the house. He didn't turn his headlights on, so no one would see him coming. As he drew closer, he could see the lights were definitely on. Every now and then he could see a light flicker, as if someone was walking between the light and the window shade. When he was about fifty yards away, he turned the engine off and let the car coast a few more feet until it rolled to a gentle stop. He didn't want to hit the brakes and have the brake lights go on.

He slowly opened the door.

The buzzer blared to alert him that the keys were still in the ignition. He quickly grabbed the keys, snatched them out, and looked up toward the house. He was probably far enough away that no one inside of the house could hear him. Nonetheless, the alarm going off was nerve-racking. He crouched down next to his patrol car, peering into Sam's place to see if anyone had been alerted to his presence.

After a moment, he felt secure enough to begin moving toward the house. Crouching down and creeping slowly closer, his heart began to beat faster. Even after years of law enforcement, the anxiety that accompanied these circumstances never disappeared. He wished he had a good swig of whiskey, but in his haste, he had left his bottle at the jail. He was now only twenty yards from the front porch. He noticed there weren't any vehicles parked out front. Either they had parked in back or had walked a long distance to get here.

With his .38-caliber pistol firmly in hand, he decided to go around back to see if he could locate a vehicle and possibly better gauge the situation. He spotted a light blue pickup and a burnt orange El Camino, which looked like Clint's car.

Phillips walked up to the El Camino and looked inside. The belongings on the seat looked familiar. He recognized the red jacket as one Clint wore during off hours. He also saw what looked to be a roll of undeveloped film laying on top of the jacket. A surge of excitement and anxiety rushed through his body as he contemplated grabbing the film. He acted on his impulse and reached down, quietly pulling the door latch up on the passenger's side. The door was locked.

"Damn it!" He whispered.

He looked through the window to the driver's side door. It appeared to be unlocked, so he crept around to that side of the car.

He looked up toward the house to see if anyone was approaching. The coast was clear, so he again tried entering the vehicle. He pulled on the latch and the door opened.

"Whew!" He said silently.

He leaned into the car and grabbed the roll of film, slipping it into his jacket pocket and looking back toward the house. He saw shadows moving in the back room. He paused for a moment. Although he didn't sense he was in physical danger, he did need to consider the often ruthless behavior exhibited by the extremists in the area.

He sensed the very real possibility these fanatics, as well as his deputy, were behind what had happened. He felt compelled to approach the house and confront the intruders. He drew his pistol again and made his way back to the front of the house. He slowly proceeded up the stairs, keeping a vigilant eye on the front window and door. He worked his way over to a window and peered in. He could see two men on the floor where Sam's body had been found.

"What the...?"

He leaned back from the window sill to figure out his next move. As he stepped back, the porch made a loud creak. Not hesitating for a moment, Sheriff Phillips jumped to the front door and crashed through it, kicking it open with his foot. His revolver drawn, aimed at the two men who were kneeling on the floor. They had been alerted to an intruder by the creaking outside and were reaching for the shotguns they had propped up against the wall.

"Hold it right there, fellas," the sheriff asserted. "Jim, Zak what the hell is going on here?" he asked, still aiming his pistol at their heads.

He heard a click, then felt the hammer of a pistol being pulled back into the firing position as it pressed against his head. He saw Zak and Jim relax. He slowly turned his head and found himself looking into the barrel of a .9mm automatic pistol. He closed his eyes in an attempt to alleviate the fear that shot through his body.

He lowered his hands to his sides. Before he could think, the voice behind the gun spoke.

"It's all right, Sheriff. They're here with me."

He heard the pistol hammer click back into the nonfiring position, and he exhaled deeply. Sheriff Phillips turned around to see it was Clint who had held the gun to his head.

"Clint, what the fuck did you do that for?"

Clint grinned devilishly. "Well, Sheriff, I didn't want to take a chance on a gunfight starting because of a misunderstanding. I was just taking control of the situation. Sorry if I scared you."

The two men who had been on the floor were now smiling.

"Okay, I understand, but what are you all doing here?"

Without hesitation, Clint began to explain. "Well, Sheriff, you know on some of the dirtier jobs I get someone to help with the cleanup. Jim and Zak here just offered to help out. 'Course, it's gonna cost the department a couple of beers, right boys?"

"That's right," they responded in unison.

Phillips took a deep breath and shook his head once, not quite relaxed yet. He looked at Clint. "Where is Margarita? Doesn't she usually do these cleanup jobs?"

"Yeah, Sheriff, she does, but she wasn't anywhere to be found when I called her."

"Clint, why the rush?"

"Well, Sheriff, I'm just trying to be efficient, that's all."

The sheriff realized he might be pushing too far and stopped his questions. He looked at Clint, who was getting a bit tense, and reassured him. "Okay, okay," Phillips said. "That pistol to my head just got me a little shaken up. Good work, Clint. I'm going to leave you guys to finish up here. I'll see you tomorrow."

The men waved good-bye. "See ya later, Sheriff."

"Sheriff, you get a good night's sleep. You've had a long day," Clint added.

Phillips turned and looked at him as he was walking out the front door. "I'll do just that, Clint."

Once Phillips was clearly out the door, Clint turned and stared at Zak and Jim. He clenched his lips tightly. "He knows."

Big Jim naively responded, "Clint, he doesn't—"

"He knows! He can't prove anything right now, but he knows. I know him too well. Right now he's sucking on his whiskey bottle trying to figure out what to do next. He's going to free that uppity nigger. He's acting different. It's like he's found some new kind of goddamn morality."

"But Clint, Sheriff always lets us get away with stuff," Jim said. "We never got in any trouble harassing the niggers before. What's different now?"

Clint was agitated by Jim's ignorance. "Well, Jim, the first thing is this ain't harassing niggers. A man was murdered—a white man! Also, whoever they convict for killing that old coot is going to get the chair. I don't know how far the sheriff is going to bend with stakes this high. He has let things slide, but he never was one of the good old boys. He just let things go to keep his job. I don't know what he's going to do now, but one thing is certain—he's up to something."

He stopped to think, then walked over to the window and watched as Sheriff Phillips' car pulled down the long drive and off Sam's property.

Zak looked at Clint as he was staring out the window, rubbing his chin. "What're we gonna do, Clint?"

When Clint turned and looked at Zak and Jim, they could see the seething hate that ran through his heart.

"We have to take them down, both of them!" Clint sneered.

Zak smiled.

Big Jim, on the other hand, was shaken. "Take them down? You mean kill 'em? Clint, I can't go through that again. What we did to old Sam was a mistake. We didn't mean for that to happen, right? I mean, the niggers deserve a little hassle every now and then, but I don't want to be no murderer."

Clint walked over to Jim and without hesitation reached up and grabbed him around the throat and started choking him. He put his face close to Jim's face and yelled, "Jim, you big dumb fuck. You are already elbows deep into murder. You were the one holding Sam when he got his throat cut. If any of us goes down, we're all goin' down. The good news for you is that we ain't goin' down. You know why? Because you're going to do exactly what I tell you to do and you are going to say exactly what I tell you to say. We need to tie up some loose ends. Then, this whole situation will be over. You know why? Because when it's over, I'll be the sheriff and that will be that. Do you understand me, boy?"

Jim just stood there with Clint still clutching him around the throat. He was sniveling like a small child who had just been scolded.

"I said, Do you understand me?"

"Yes, sure Clint," Jim responded timidly. "Anything you say. I didn't understand before—okay."

Lake let go and Jim straightened himself up. Clint then turned towards the remaining mess on the floor. "Now let's hurry and get this place cleaned up. We have a lot to do."

22.

Sheriff Phillips returned to the station a little before two a.m. Sunday morning. He walked briskly into the office and found Lance still on duty, sitting at his desk reading a newspaper.

"Lance, I've got to develop some film. Don't let anyone disturb me, including Clint."

"Sure, Sheriff, but don't you want to tell me what's going on?"

"There's no time, Lance. Just stay on your toes."

Phillips went into the tiny room they used as a crime lab and started to work immediately.

The roll contained nine images from the Sam Stinson crime scene. Phillips made hard copies from the negatives of each one. Adjusting the light so he could see better, he quickly looked through all the pictures. Nothing jumped out at him. He went back through and studied the pictures a second and even a third time. There was nothing out of the ordinary. He was baffled and wondered why Clint would have gone to the trouble to take the film. What was he hiding? He put his forehead in his hands in exasperation. Rubbing his head, he muttered, "Why? Why?"

He leaned back in the desk chair in the corner of the little room and thumbed through the photos once more. He was being very careful, examining every detail. He studied the last picture meticulously, then shook his head. Nothing, he thought. These were basic crime scene photos. Why would Clint take them?

He put the pictures down on a table and sat back down in the chair. Hands clasped behind his head, the sheriff stretched his legs out and leaned way back in the chair. He told himself to relax. He stayed in that position for awhile, looking around the office and running the day's events through his head. Then he looked down at his shoes. He could see the dried mud hanging off the sides. He sat upright so he could get a closer look at his shoes.

He jumped up and ran over to the pictures. He frantically flipped through them until he got to the two pictures of Sam lying on the floor. He pulled them out and looked at them under the magnifying glass. As he examined the blood-stained area around Sam's body, he could see traces of footprints. He doubled the magnification. He could clearly see a pattern. He also recalled that he and Clint had put plastic booties over their shoes before they entered the crime scene. The booties were used to preserve the integrity of the crime scene, so their prints would not be mistaken for the footprints made when the crime was committed.

"Lance. Lance," he cried out, studying the pictures, magnifying them yet again. He heard a knock on the lab door.

"Lance," the sheriff yelled through the door.

Lance responded from the other side, realizing he should never walk into the lab without first verifying it was safe to enter and not ruin exposures.

"Yeah, Sheriff. Are you all right in there?"

"Yes, Lance. I'm fine," he responded. "Lance, go to the cell block and get Adam Freeman out of C-10."

"Right away, Sheriff."

He could hear Lance's footsteps fading away as he walked down the hallway. He went back to work making prints of the enlarged images that contained the legible, bloody footprints.

After a while, there was a knock on the door.

"Sheriff, I have Freeman right here," Lance announced.

"Good work, Lance. Now go down into personal belongings and bring out everything marked with his name."

After Sheriff Phillips gave Lance his directive, he reached into a satchel and pulled out a small bottle. He affectionately looked at the bottle in his hand and took a swig.

"Ah!" he sighed as the pleasure of his Kentucky whiskey took the edge off his tension.

He finished the second of the two prints and walked out the lab door to see Adam sitting on the bench in the main office area. He stood over Adam holding the eight-by-eleven-inch prints in his right hand.

"Adam, was there ever anyone else with you and Sam in his house?"

Adam didn't hesitate for a moment. "No!"

"Are you sure the story you told me is the truth?" the sheriff asked again.

"Yes," he said confidently. "Now, do you want to tell me what is going on and how long—"

"How many pairs of shoes did you bring on your trip, son?"

Adam, a bit puzzled, looked up at him. "Two. Why?"

Lance walked into the room carrying Adam's bags that had been confiscated earlier by Deputy Lake.

"Adam, hold up the bottoms of your shoes."

Adam was reluctant as well as confused. "What?"

"Show me the bottoms of your goddamn shoes. Take them off—now—damn it."

"Okay," Adam responded timidly.

He took off his shoes and handed them to Sheriff Phillips. Phillips turned the shoes over to look at the bottoms. He held the enlarged photo that had the detailed footprints up next to Adam's shoes. The pattern on Adam's shoes clearly did not match the ones in the picture.

"Lance, look in his bag and find any other pairs of shoes."

Lance did what Sheriff Phillips asked. After a couple of minutes, he held up two pairs of dress shoes, both with completely smooth bottoms. Phillips let out a sigh. It was hard to tell whether his reaction signified disappointment or relief. Again, he took a deep breath and sighed.

"Lance, prepare a set of release documents. We've got the wrong man."

23.

Adam closed the door to the squad car. He leaned down and thanked Lance for the ride and bid him farewell.

"You take care and try to get out of here as soon as you can," Lance said.

Adam, knowing Lance meant well, shook his head and stepped back from the car as it pulled away.

He was standing in the Thompsons' driveway at three o'clock on a Sunday morning. He wondered if he would be better off waking the Thompsons and staying the rest of the night there, or if he should just move on. He looked up at Marlena's bedroom window and his heartbeat quickened. He took a deep breath as he remembered that first night together—the walk around the garden, the way they had shared their thoughts with each other, their first kiss.

He half smiled and chuckled as he filled with the emotion and pride a man feels when he reminisces about a love that was once his. Remembering the beauty of such a love was often bittersweet. For, also present in his heart, was the pain of losing that love and being faced with the harsh realization that the one his heart claimed as his own was never really his. Instead, this love had presented him with bitter disappointment.

The temptation to see Marlena again drove Adam to approach the large porch at the front of the house. Slowly, he walked up the stairs, contemplating what he would say. He stood staring at the door, trying to gain enough courage to knock.

He stepped back off the porch and gazed longingly at her window. He shook his head. "I can't do it," he whispered to himself.

He picked up his bag and walked to his rental car, still parked in the driveway. He unlocked the door, threw in his things, and got in. After one last glance, he started the car, put it in gear, and drove off.

Adam pulled up in front of the First Baptist Church. He got out of the car and made his way up the massive set of stairs leading to the entrance. He pulled on the door, but it was locked.

"Shit!"

He caught himself, realizing the inappropriateness of the expletive he'd just used on these holy grounds. Looking up at the cross on top of the steeple, he said, "Oh, excuse me. I didn't mean anything."

He walked around to the rear of the church to see if he could find an open door. He passed a door on the side of the building, which he tried without success. Continuing to the rear of the church, he noticed a car in a small parking lot. He also noticed there was a light on in one of the rooms at the back of the building. He excitedly walked to the rear door and tried to open it, but it too was locked. He backed up to get a better view of the lit window. He could see a shadow moving. Someone was there.

He knocked at the door, desperately hoping to receive refuge from Eve's streets. He heard a man's voice telling him to hold on, followed by the sound of footsteps descending a flight of stairs and approaching the door. There was a brief fumbling with the dead bolt from the inside and the door opened.

There stood Reverend Jacobson. At first he seemed startled, but his expression quickly turned to joy when he realized his newfound friend had been released.

"I didn't know where else to go," Adam said quietly.

The reverend flashed him a warm glowing smile. "Well, son, you came to the right place…. and the children of the Father returned home, to live forever in his glory," he finished, quoting scripture.

It had been a while since Adam had attended a church service, so he felt a bit uncomfortable. He did, however, recognize the quote and recited its location back to the reverend. The reverend was pleased and smiled again, putting Adam at ease.

"Come in. Come in," Jacobson said gesturing. "So, they cut you loose, huh? Praise be. How long you been out?"

"Must be an hour now," Adam answered.

"So, this must be the first place you've been."

"Well, the deputy dropped me off at my car, which was still at the Thompsons'. But yeah, other than that I haven't been anywhere else."

"Smart move, son," the reverend replied. "You need to let this situation cool off. Stay around these parts where it's safe and by all means, stay away from that white girl."

"But, Reverend—"

"But nothin', son. You got yourself neck-deep in some awful shit. If you know what's best, you will stay as far away from her as you can, until you get yourself out of here. As much as I want to try and convince you to stick around and be a role model, I know the best thing for both you and this town is to get you as far away from here, as fast as possible."

The two men were now in the church kitchen. Adam was sitting at a small table while the reverend stood across from him. For a while they were both silent. Then the reverend offered Adam a cup of coffee.

"No," Adam answered. "I am really tired. Is there anywhere I can take a nap?"

"Yes, of course, right this way."

Reverend Jacobson showed Adam to a small room down the hall from his office.

As Adam followed the reverend into the room he noticed a small cot in the corner.

"It is a bit small," the reverend said, "but it should serve you pretty well. I use it myself on those long days and nights when I need to catch a few winks to refresh myself."

He reached into a closet and grabbed a blanket. "If you get chilly, you can use this," he said as he laid the blanket across the cot.

Adam sat down on the modest bed as Reverend Jacobson left the room. It was a little flimsy, but at this point he was just grateful to have a place to lay down as a free man.

Reverend Jacobson popped his head back through the door and said, "Oh yeah, Adam, if you aren't awake by nine, I just want to forewarn you this place is going to be rockin'.'"

Adam lay back with his head on his pillow reflecting on the past two days. He could feel the medallion Sam had given him about to slide out of his pant pocket. He reached down and grabbed it. Looking at it caused him to wonder. Could it be possible? That man—Lieutenant Jefferson, died the day he lost it. Sam gave it away and was found dead the next day. Coincidence? Adam felt a surge of energy run through his body. Coincidence, maybe, but he was not going to risk it. He clutched the medallion close to his chest silently vowing to never let it out of his sight.

24.

Sheriff Phillips was giving Lance instructions relating to the apprehension of Lake, Zak, and big Jim. If seen, they were to be considered armed and dangerous and should be taken into custody immediately.

"Lance, I understand this puts you in an awkward position. Do you think you can go through with arresting Clint?"

Lance answered confidently, almost too confidently, "Of course, Sheriff. You can count on me."

Phillips pressed his lips tightly together and shook his head, saying, "God, I hate having to do this, but we had better get a move on. It's getting close to seven a.m."

Sheriff Phillips strapped on his holster, checked his ammunition belt, and pulled out his revolver to make sure it was loaded. Just as he was sliding the pistol back in his holster, in walked Clint, still in his clothes from the day before.

"Morning, Sheriff," he said cheerfully. "How's our prisoner doing?"

"He's gone, Clint," Phillips answered curtly. "We released him early this morning."

Clint stood perfectly calm, seemingly unfazed by the news. "That sure was fast, Sheriff. What happened?" Clint asked.

Phillips' forehead began to bead with perspiration as he felt the tension build. Clint reached over and grabbed an apple off the sheriff's desk, still waiting for a response to his question. Lance subtly placed his hand close to his pistol.

Phillips looked directly into Clint's eyes. "Clint, he didn't do it."

"So, what are you guys up to?" Clint asked, his tone a bit sarcastic.

Phillips looked over at Lance and said, "Well, Clint, as a matter of fact, we were about to come looking for you. Have a seat."

"Well, Tom, I really need to get going. I just came by to pick up the film from the crime scene. I think I left it here yesterday."

Phillips reached down and grabbed a large manila folder off his desk. He reached in and slid the contents out. He held them up so Clint could see they were the crime scene photos. "Clint, I think you'd better have a seat."

Without a word, Clint turned and dashed for the door. Both Sheriff Phillips and Lance took off after him. As Clint threw the door open, Lance dove and tackled him. They both tumbled out the door and landed on the porch outside the jail.

"Cuff him," Sheriff Phillips commanded.

After restraining Clint with handcuffs, Lance brought him back inside and sat him down next to the sheriff's desk. Phillips then told Lance to take off Clint's shoes, which Lance promptly did. He handed them to the sheriff, who took the shoes and laid them upside down on his desk so that he could see the treads. Grabbing the enlarged photos from the crime scene, Phillips compared the two.

"That's it!" he exclaimed. "They match."

Lance took a deep breath and Clint sat there tightening his lips and breathing heavily.

"Where are Zak and Jim?" Sheriff Phillips asked.

Clint sat silently, not responding.

Phillips firmly clenched Clint's face in his hand and looked him square in the eyes. "I said, where are Zak and Jim?"

Clint still just sat there, silent.

Sheriff Phillips turned to Lance. "Lance, read him his rights. I've got to go and see if I can locate those two before the Blossom Festival parade. I think there's going to be trouble today if I don't. Where did you drop Adam off?"

Lance answered, "Well, I took him to his car, which was over at the Thompsons'. I don't know if he stayed there or not."

The sheriff nodded, "Okay, I'll try there first. You lock him up and stay put. I'll get back here as soon as possible."

There was a vigorous bang at the door.

Sara Thompson turned toward Marlena. "I wonder who that could be."

Marlena shook her head as she continued to sew the colorful costume she was to wear in the town's Blossom Festival parade later that morning.

When Sara opened the door, she was a bit startled. "Sheriff Phillips. What brings you here? We were just getting ready to go to the jail and see Adam. How is he?" she asked with concern.

Sheriff Phillips politely replied, "Well, Mrs. Thompson, I'm here looking for Adam. I see his car is gone. I wondered if you knew his whereabouts."

Marlena briskly walked toward the doorway where Sara and the sheriff were standing. "Did he escape?"

"No, Marlena. We released him early this morning. We've discovered some compelling evidence that pretty much absolves Adam of murdering Sam. We do believe, however, that he may be in danger."

Sara mumbled, "I thought he would stay here—that he would feel safe with us."

Marlena stood there looking out at where Adam's car had been parked in the driveway. Every feeling she had for him ran through her heart. She knew she loved him and feared she would lose him, either to his own fear, or to the violence this town had spawned.

She knew why he hadn't stayed at their house when he was released. He couldn't bear to see her. He couldn't stand the tension and danger involved with loving her. His love for her wasn't enough to call forward the valor and courage she knew resided deep within his soul. It was the same valor that had driven him to achieve what he had thus far in his life, the same passion she saw him express to little Ricky, the courage that kept him alive through the crash that fateful night he arrived in Eve. She saw all of these things in him, but he couldn't or wouldn't call on them now to make real this love they shared.

She stood there in the doorway, her eyes filling with tears as she wondered if she would ever see him again. She hoped for this, if for no other reason than to say good-bye and gaze into his eyes one last time. He couldn't hide his feelings from her there. When one loved truly, there is no room for doubt, no place for worry. All that one felt was the present moment with all its joy, its sorrow. There was a direct correlation between the amount of joy and pain one could feel. If you held back your heart so you will not feel love's pain, you could never truly feel all of love's joy.

Marlena experienced the truth of this in her heart, and in doing so her love was blind. Adam could have been of any descent and it wouldn't have changed the way she felt. In this moment, all she knew was how absolutely ecstatic being with Adam could make her. She knew by looking into her own heart and feeling the depth of her sorrow.

25.

"We shall overcome, we shall overcome, when the Lord returns, we shall be rejoicin', when the Lord comes."

Adam bolted up in bed, startled by the voices that rang through the church and reverberated around the small room where he was sleeping. He looked around groggily, trying to figure out where he was. Then he remembered coming to the church last night. He also recalled the warning Reverend Jacobson had given him before he drifted off to sleep. This had to be the "rockin'" Reverend Jacobson had referred to.

He got up from the small cot and made his way to the washroom across the hall. He did a quick job of cleaning up and returned to his room. His clothes were crumpled from having slept in them and he made a half-hearted effort at straightening himself up before deciding to make his way toward the raucous noises coming from below.

As he worked his way down the back stairs, his spirits began to lift from the infectiousness of the jubilant singing coming from inside the sanctuary. It engulfed his soul and he felt a surge of energy.

Adam remembered the days of his childhood when he attended the Baptist church with his father back in Detroit. The singing was always his favorite part of those Sunday visits. Unfortunately, it was everything else that turned him away from this sort of religious worship. The hellfire and damnation that came from the bullying pulpit, the two-and-a-half-hour sermons no one seemed to be able to stay awake through, and the pressure to fit a preconceived mold and be someone he was not. He couldn't take it.

Yes, it had certainly been a while since he had found himself in a church such as this. But on this occasion, he felt a real sense of salvation and knew he was where he truly belonged, if for no other reason than it seemed to be the only place in the area where he was welcomed or of which the community approved.

As he made his way down the hallway leading to the sanctuary, the intensity of the vibration increased. Indeed, the whole place was rockin'. He worried about his appearance, then rationalized that if he entered in the rear of the sanctuary and quickly sat down, no one would notice him.

He reached the doors as the rhythm of the gospel was escalating to a feverish pitch. He peered through the narrow windows on the door. The choir wore bright red robes with purple trim. They were swaying back and forth with the rhythm of their verse, while the entire congregation rocked in unison. It seemed as if the building itself joined in the vacillating movement.

There were people dancing in the aisles and nurses rushing to the aid of those who were too feeble to hold up in the experience of such rapture. He smiled as vivid memories from his childhood began to flood his consciousness. He had been here before, or at least in a place just like it. He felt comfortable enough to open the door and go inside.

When he pulled the door open, the full force of the room jolted him. He hadn't realized how much of a dampening effect the door had provided. Now he was standing in the full force of the resounding voices and boisterous ecstasy of the congregation.

He stood just inside the door as it closed behind him. There were a few empty seats in the last two rows. As he made his way into the last row, he looked up toward the pulpit and saw three men sitting there. They were vibrating in their chairs, clapping their hands, and shaking their heads to the cadence of the music.

Just as Adam sat down, one of the men sitting next to Reverend Jacobson noticed him. He nodded in approval, then nudged the reverend to point Adam out. The man motioned toward where Adam was sitting and Adam and the reverend made eye contact. Reverend Jacobson beamed a wonderful smile at Adam and, like the other gentleman, gave a gesture of approval.

The church sanctuary continued to rock, as the reverend put it. Adam sat there, thoroughly entertained by all of the pageantry and excitement around him.

A woman two rows ahead of him suddenly leapt from her seat and began writhing wildly. He could hear her shouting, although it seemed incoherent. He remembered this phenomenon from his childhood as "speaking in tongues." After a moment the woman passed out and two elderly women dressed in nurses' garb rushed to her aid. As the music began to subside, Adam relaxed. Looking around the church, he noticed what seemed like a thousand hand-held fans being shaken briskly by the women holding them. The smell of perfume and cologne permeated the room, for everyone was in their very best attire.

There was a sad beauty in what Adam was experiencing. The uplifting of the human spirit in the face of life circumstances that reeked of debasement. What they didn't realize was they didn't have to spend their lives like this. They didn't have to tolerate the oppression that had held dominion over their lives for generations. They just didn't see another way to cope.

To live a life of obedience, in order to reap the rewards granted in the hereafter—for Adam it seemed a tragic waste of human potential. It also struck him that this belief was fuel for the oppression that had kept them financially stagnant for so long.

As the gospel faded, the only sound was the organ humming the melody of the song the choir had just finished singing.

Murmurs of "Oh yeah" and "Praise Jesus" could be heard throughout the sanctuary. Soon a poignant voice began to ring out.

"In thee, O Lord, do I take refuge; Let me never be put to shame!

In thy righteousness deliver me and rescue me; inline thy ear to me, and save me!"

The reverend paused long enough to wipe the sweat from his brow with his white cotton handkerchief. "Be thou to me a rock of refuge, a strong fortress, to save me, for thou art my rock and my fortress."

"Preach it, reverend. Oh yes!" someone shouted from the congregation.

Reverend Jacobson turned toward Adam, looking at him directly. "Rescue me, O my God, from the hand of the wicked, from the grasp of the unjust and cruel man. For thou, O Lord, art my hope, my trust, O Lord, from my youth."

The reverend finished by raising his hand up in a fist, shaking it ferverently towards the heavens. The congregation was thundering with approval. Still looking at Adam the reverend nodded at him and smiled.

It was ironic that Reverend Jacobson was quoting these particular words of scripture, for they seemed to address the very thoughts Adam was having. Again, the congregation became stirred up as Jacobson moved them with his wisdom and conveyance of the "Lord's words."

Adam glanced around the room. About ten rows up and to the right of the center aisle, he noticed Teri. She, too, was nodding her head in agreement with the reverend's words. She turned and looked at Adam, seeming to know exactly where he was. It was as if he were in that very same seat every week. The glance she gave him out of the corner of her eye was mesmerizing. She wore a black hat trimmed in white, so he could just see her eyes underneath the brim. She gave him a warm, accepting smile.

She seemed more beautiful than the first time he had seen her, and the warmth of her smile put him at ease. They held each other's gaze for a moment, then continued to listen to the reverend's inspiring sermon.

Reverend Jacobson began talking about Eve's recent

turmoil and the misgivings the town's law enforcement had about their unexpected visitor. He went on about the religious symbolism involved with the events and how its retribution was quickly served. Adam began to get uneasy, especially when the reverend seemed to be heading toward an introduction.

"Now here was a man of great achievement. He had flown some of America's most important men all over the world."

"Yea!" someone in the congregation exclaimed.

"When he arrived in our midst, he was on his way to make even better for himself, by purchasing his own airport. Here is a man that can serve as an inspiration and role model to us all."

"Well!" came another affirmation from the congregation.

"Maybe, if we show him a proper First Baptist welcome, we can get him to stick around a little while, and teach us, some things. Brothers and sisters, let us give a wholehearted welcome to our waylaid, black airman, Mr. Adam Freeman."

The congregation began to cheer wildly. Adam was deeply moved, as well as embarrassed. The congregation continued to applaud as Reverend Jacobson motioned for him to rise. He looked at Teri, who smiled proudly at him and nodded, also gesturing for him to rise and accept this loving gift.

As Adam stood, blushing, Reverend Jacobson went on, "Brothers and sisters, I have learned that Brother Adam has already seen the potential for one of our own to accomplish great things, as we can see by his fine example. All it takes is support and the proper tutelage."

Adam sat back in his seat. As he did, an older gentleman sitting right in front of him turned around and held out his hand for a handshake.

"God bless you, son. Welcome to First Baptist," the man said with a very deep drawl.

Adam smiled and thanked the older man as Jacobson went on with his sermon. When the sermon began winding down, Reverend Jacobson made some general announcements. He spent a considerable amount of time reminding the parishioners of their specific tasks for the Blossom Festival parade and activities that were to begin later that morning.

When he had concluded, the lively music started up and continued as the congregation filed out of the sanctuary. Everyone continued to clap their hands and sing until they were out on the front steps. Reverend Jacobson stood outside on the steps shaking hands with everyone who walked past.

"Thank you, Reverend Jacobson, that was a beautiful sermon," they all seemed to say.

"May they Lord be with you today and always, sister," he would reply.

One of the older women asked, "Do you really think he'll stick around for awhile?"

"We'll have to wait and see, sister," the reverend said.

Adam waited a while before entering the steady stream of people exiting the aisles. As he sat in his seat waiting, several people spoke to him, wishing him well and welcoming him to their church. He looked around and tried to spot Teri, but it seemed she had already left the sanctuary. Finally, he stood up and made his way outside, following the stream of people. The line of well-wishers in front of Reverend Jacobson was dwindling, but he was spending more time talking with each person, so the line wasn't moving any faster. Reverend Jacobson looked down the line and caught a glimpse of Adam patiently waiting, so he sped things along.

"Praise the Lord, son. I'm glad you could join us this morning. I wondered if you would make it down," the reverend said smiling.

Adam smiled back at him. "Now, Reverend Jacobson, do you really expect me to believe you had any doubt I would make it to church with all that racket going on right beneath me? I bet you told that fine choir of yours to sing twice as loud as usual this morning."

The two men chuckled. Reverend Jacobson nodded. "I warned you, son, and I said no such thing to our wonderful choir. No sir, it wasn't me." The reverend looked up to the heavens as he finished his statement, implying divine intervention.

"Hello, Mr. Freeman," came a small voice.

Adam looked down and there stood Ricky, the boy he'd met in Marlena's classroom. Ricky smiled up at Adam. "Mr. Freeman, I made something for you."

In his hand was a picture he had drawn. He held it out for Adam.

Adam took the picture and expressed his genuine thanks. He looked at the picture and was touched. It was a crayon drawing of a man flying an airplane over a steeple that resembled the one at the church.

Ricky went on to explain his drawing. "Mr. Freeman, it's a picture of you flying away from here after you get your airplane all fixed. It's sort of like a good luck picture."

"Come here Ricky, and quit botherin' that man," came a stern voice as an unkempt looking woman walked up and grabbed the boy by the arm. The woman looked at Adam and smiled, somewhat flirtatiously. "I tell him not to bother folks, but the boy just doesn't listen."

"The boy was bothering no one, Josa. This is a fine boy you have here," Reverend Jacobson said affectionately as he put his arm around Ricky to ease him.

"Good morning, Airman Freeman. So glad to have you join us here at First Baptist this morning."

Adam looked over to see who was giving the greeting. Approaching the stairs to the church was Teri. She gave Adam an engaging smile. He couldn't help his eyes wandering down to her fitted white dress. Every curve was apparent and moved just as she did—with purpose. Adam wondered how can the Lord let her get away with wearing that to church. That had to be a sin. He knew the thoughts that he was having were.

He smiled back at her and raised his eyebrows. "Good morning, Ms. Jones. You are looking very well this morning." He made sure not to overstate his compliment and cause a stir.

"It's good to see you a free man again, Adam. Some of us were worried about you," she said.

"Well, Teri, that makes two of us."

"Well now," the reverend interupted, "we have a lot to get accomplished if we are going to be ready for this morning's parade. Will you be joining the festivities today, Adam?"

"Well, I really hadn't planned on it, Reverend. I don't—"

"Come on, Adam," Teri said, "you can be my personal guest. After all, what else are you going to do on a beautiful day like this?"

"What do you say, Adam?" The Reverend added. "Take a day here and have some fun."

"What the heck," Adam said, feeling swept up in the moment.

They all smiled and Teri offered to swing by and pick Adam up in an hour, so they could walk over to Main Street together and watch the parade.

The mood turned quickly when the sheriff's car pulled up in front of the church. Deputy Lance and another man dressed in civilian clothes got out of the squad car. The civilian man wore blue jeans and a denim button-down shirt. He stood about six feet tall and had dusty-blond hair. The man's rugged good looks made Adam think he must have been one of the locals. The two men approached him.

Lance raised his hand, gesturing to his companion. "Here he is."

Noticing the baffled look on Adam's face, Lance said, "I guess you've never been formally introduced to your mechanic. Mike, this is Adam."

The group sighed a collective breath of relief. Lance went on to explain that the circumstances that led to Adam's arrest had been deteriorating and the sheriff feared for the safety of everyone involved. That was the reason Mike was given a police escort to find Adam.

The news caused a bit of a stir. The last thing this town needed was another reason to hate. It was bad enough as it was. Fortunately, the only ones privy to this information were those standing with Adam—Teri and Reverend Jacobson.

They both understood the sensitivity of the situation. If tension in the community were to rise because of some circumstance on either side, it could trigger a riot, like back in 1978.

That incident had been set off by rumors of a black teenage boy having raped a white girl. The town responded with four days of rioting that left seven people dead and scores injured. The teenage boy was later found lynched in a field outside of town.

Both Teri and Reverend Jacobson were apprehensive that the current conditions could yield similar results. Although unspoken, each knew they had the same concern. The best thing to do was to keep everything as quiet as possible until the entire dilemma had been sorted out. As much as they both wanted to see Adam stick around, for his sake and that of the community, it was probably best for him to leave as quickly as possible.

Maybe he could return on occasion to serve as a mentor for the black children in Eve. The reverend had this visitation plan pretty well mapped out. Teri was thinking along the same lines. Ironically, not a word of this well-devised proposition had been mentioned to Adam.

"Adam, it's great to finally meet you," Mike said as he reached out to shake Adam's hand. "Jarrell told me a lot about you. Well, anyway, there's some good news and some not-so-good news about your plane."

You could see the tension quickly develop in Adam's stance as he waited for the prognosis.

"Adam, the good news is your engine and all of your electrical and vacuum systems sustained only minor damage, most of which I was able to correct yesterday. You had said earlier that you ran out of fuel, but there was plenty in both tanks. My guess is that your carb iced up and killed your engine after you lowered your rpm's. Everything in your engine is checking out fine. Also, since I knew about your prop beforehand, I brought one with me and was able to replace it. I've put it through a series of high-rev tests and it held up pretty well. However, there's a bit of structural damage that needs to be addressed. I'm going to have to replace your cowling. There is also damage to the left wing tip and the landing gear has been knocked out of alignment. I'm getting a warning light on your gear retracting system and I wasn't able to ascertain whether your landing gear is working or not. I can fly down to New Orleans and get the parts. I'm planning on starting on the remaining work tomorrow."

Adam, grateful that the news did not seem too catastrophic, smiled. "How long do you think it'll take?"

Mike thought briefly. "Well, if all goes smoothly, two or three days, and that's a push. I usually give myself a week to ten days for a job like this. I understand your circumstances, so that is what I'm planning. The deputy here has offered some protection while I work, so I need to get done as soon as I can."

"Well, that isn't exactly what I wanted to hear, but it's also not the worst news I could get. Look, Mike, thanks. I really appreciate all you're doing. I know this isn't an ordinary job. If I can get up to the Northwest and close the deal in Friday Harbor, I want you to know you have a job there, if you want it."

The two smiled and shook hands. Mike said good-bye and left with Lance. Adam watched them as they drove away. He smiled, feeling things might finally be changing. His journey to the Northwest was finally getting back on track. He asked Reverend Jacobson if there was a phone nearby. He had to call his financial backer and the gentleman who was selling the airport to give them an update on his arrival.

Adam's excitement was obvious and everyone present was touched by it. There was something magical about witnessing a man going through the process of living out his dreams. It seemed to give hope to them all.

26.

Adam heard a knock at the door and looked at his watch wondering who it could be. He didn't expect Teri to swing by for another twenty minutes. Besides, he was supposed to meet her in front of the church. It must be Reverend Jacobson, he thought. He hurried to the door, his shirt unbuttoned.

To his surprise, there stood Marlena. She smiled coyly and said, "Hello, Adam. I heard they released you last night. Sheriff Phillips told us you were probably here, and I just wanted to see how you were doing."

Adam was flabbergasted. As he stood there listening to her, his heart filled with every ounce of passion he possessed. Looking into her eyes, he was reminded of all the warm and tender feelings he had for her that first evening they shared. Her hair was pulled back and he could clearly see every detail of her beautiful face. She wore a white dress that draped freely. As she stood there, the gentle breeze blew the soft fabric and made it dance around her alluring frame. To Adam, she was the picture of unblemished beauty.

Although her physical beauty was undeniable, this attraction went far deeper. Without even the slightest physical touch, he felt their spirits embrace. It was as if he had known her for 10,000 years.

Adam was deathly afraid of this feeling, for to truly open himself to such love would also make him vulnerable to the unbearable pain he felt was imminent. As a man, he was not unfamiliar with these feelings, but to risk acting on them was quite another proposition.

Adam gathered himself and greeted Marlena as coolly as he could manage. "Hi, Marlena. Yeah, I was going to come by later and thank you and your parents for all you've done for me. I really appreciate you folks a lot."

"No trouble at all. As a matter of fact, my mom asked me to let you know that if you ever need a place to stay, you are welcome in our home. She also asked me to give you this." She reached out her hand with a present.

"What's this?"

"I don't know. Maybe you should open it."

She smiled as he looked down at her. Adam's heart was heavy. He felt the hopelessness of never being able to sustain a relationship with this woman—the love of his life.

He opened the package and found a book entitled *The Prophet,* by Kahlil Gibran.

"Wow. I've heard a lot about this book."

He opened it to the inscription on the inside cover.

Adam, this is wonderful reading for quiet times. If you are like me, it may hold the key to some of life's challenging questions. You are a credit to the human race, and if I were to ever have a son, I would hope he would turn out exactly like you. With love, Sara Thompson.

He stood there quietly. If he weren't such a male, he would have succumbed to his emotions and cried the tears welling up inside. Instead, he looked away and fought them off.

"Man, Marlena, this is one of the nicest things anyone has ever said about me," he finally said.

"Well, whatever it is, you probably deserve it." She smiled at him as she reached up and gently stroked his cheek. "Adam, are you doing all right? I was so worried about you."

Adam reached up and took Marlena's hand in his. He gently began to squeeze it, as if this were all the hug he could allow himself. He closed his eyes for a moment, holding her hand to his cheek. Opening them again, he looked down at her. "Marlena, I really do think the world of you. When I think of all of the crazy things that have happened to me in the last few days, there's one thing that's painfully clear. That is, you're one very special woman. I often wish something could come of us. I mean, that night at your parent's house was the best night of my life, but practically speaking, we could never make this work. There is too much against us."

She looked up at him and asked curtly, "Like what?"

Not expecting the question, Adam was silent for a moment.

"Marlena, you surprise me sometimes. I mean, really, look at where we're at and all the things that have happened to us, particularly me, over the last couple of days. This country just isn't ready for interracial relationships. People would be trying to make it hard for us from now on."

Marlena looked at Adam steadily. "Is that it?"

Again, he was thrown off guard. "I'm a pilot and I'm gone a lot—that surely wouldn't help." Her coolness was beginning to agitate Adam.

"I thought you were going to be more of an administrator at your airport in Friday Harbor." She raised her eyebrows and smiled devilishly at him, knowing she had his number.

"Marlena, you don't seem to understand how many—"

"Adam, stop. Look at me. Look into my eyes."

He did as she asked, and as he did, deep down he wanted nothing more than to grab her, hold her tight, and never let go.

She could see it in his eyes. As much as she wanted to fight for him, she didn't want the burden of dragging him someplace he didn't want to go. His love for her was apparent.

Marlena had been given the confirmation she was seeking. If Adam chose not to be with her, she knew it had nothing to do with how he actually felt. His love for her was gloriously clear. She reached up to kiss him and he turned away.

"Marlena, I can't. As much as I want to, I don't want you to be hurt any more than you already have been. I don't want to lead you to believe we have a chance, when I feel like we don't."

She looked down, feeling dejected. She had so hoped he would come around. As tears welled up in her eyes, she turned her head and wiped away a single tear that had managed to make its way down her cheek. She gathered herself and looked back up at Adam.

"Well, I guess that's it, then." She then added, "We have a spot in town square for the Blossom Festival picnic. Mom and Dad wanted me to invite you to eat with us. You're welcome to join us if you'd like. Don't worry, though, I'll keep my distance. You also don't need to feel obligated. They'll understand if you're not comfortable with it."

She gave him a half-hearted smile, then turned and walked away. As she walked out the door, the tears streamed down her cheeks. She struggled to keep from completely breaking down and crying out loud.

He called after her down the hallway, "Marlena. Marlena."

She didn't respond. She just faded away down the stairs and out of his life.

As she approached the front exit, she could hear people talking outside. She stopped in the foyer to dry her eyes and gain her composure before leaving the building. When she walked out onto the porch, Teri was standing there talking to one of the elders. They both looked at Marlena and bid her farewell.

Although Marlena had taken the time to dry her tears, her pain was evident. She quickened her pace to her car and drove away.

27.

The mood was festive all around Eve. There were cars decorated as parade floats making last-minute adjustments and gathering at the foot of Main Street on the southern edge of town.

Clowns were running about, and there were horsemen, jugglers, and characters with oversized heads. The glorious day of the Eve Blossom Festival had arrived and there wasn't a soul who would miss it. Eve's high school marching band members were warming up their instruments, blaring an occasional note. Someone had even coaxed the Shreveport Community College band to come down and strut their stuff. This was by far Eve's biggest single event of the year.

The irony was that even with all of the electricity in the air and the joy on the surface of this gala event, the town remained split, divided by a color line. All of the preparations for the parade made by whites were done on their side of town—the west side. The blacks completed their preparations on the east.

Traditionally, blacks and whites alternated floats down the parade route. However, at the conclusion of the route, the white entrants made a left turn and headed to Town Square for their annual picnic in Washington Park. Conversely, the blacks exited to the right with their floats, headed for King Park and the annual black celebration. To witness the separation of the two groups at the end of an event so uniting in spirit was indeed bizarre. How could people share so much love in one instant and then return to some artificial separation because of an age-old code that had gone unchecked?

All too often, views were held without question, simply because that's the way it had always been. These views became cankerous blisters that festered and ultimately ruptured into violent insurrections, leaving pain and misery in their wake.

This Blossom Day Festival was not unlike those before it. Adam's decision to no longer see Marlena was timely and spared him the further uneasiness of having to chose which side of the tracks to spend the day on. Anyway, he would probably be shunned by the majority of the whites if he had picnicked with the Thompsons. On the other hand, if he and Marlena had worked through their feelings, the desire in his heart to see her would be overwhelming. As it was now, to be around her would only be awkward, but it didn't change his longing for her. He was unsettled because the decision to not see Marlena was not driven by what his heart was telling him was true. It was, instead, the product of generations of socialization, oppression of the will to free itself from a dictatorship of reason.

Something in Adam knew he didn't stand a chance of happiness with Marlena, if left to the rationalizing of his intellectual mind. Truly, there was only one force to be relied upon to overcome ages of accumulated self-doubt, hate, and fear. It was a force accessible to every man, woman, and child, that force deep within that called out in dreams. It beckoned the dreamer to follow, not without pain, but in spite of it. For its rewards shone gloriously through all pain, all obstacles, all discomfort. It was the force that made people whole, that connected all as one.

There is never an absence of love. It is only fear turned to hate that makes it seem so. Some chose to turn their backs on love and then curse the world for her barrenness, when all they need do is turn back, and receive the gift so incredibly offered.

Adam had succumbed to this fear, his innermost dreams now nightmares. He was walking free, but not truly liberated because he had thrown away his dreams for comfort and approval. There were things worth dying for, and Adam had always believed that to be true to one's dreams was one of them. Without a dream there was nothing, no purpose. Without purpose, there was no life. What he witnessed in the cities everywhere were masses of people whose fear had carved them a niche in life, a comfortable routine with no purpose. These were not people manifesting the glory of God on earth. They had passed on every opportunity to experience their true nature, fearful it would make them different, that the risk involved was too much.

Eve was a town that served as a prime example of this phenomenon. On a day of such incredible celebration as this day, there were still people trapped in their fear of one another, and Adam found himself also being caught in the mire. He experienced the boundaries created by fear and the sense of limitation.

Adam was certainly not ashamed of spending the day with people he identified with. The shame he felt came from not being strong enough to act on what he knew to be true in his innermost heart—feelings that told him he loved Marlena as much as a man could love a woman. He wanted to be with her both now and for as long as she would have him.

He realized Teri was probably waiting for him. He quickly finished readying himself and headed off to meet her. He was excited about getting better acquainted with Teri, but his feelings just weren't the same as those for Marlena. Not only was there intense passion and magic, but Marlena had a way of melting his emotional walls. With each negative experience through the years the walls had grown thicker, yet in one brief moment, she had been able to obliterate any barrier from his awareness and he let go. He experienced what it was like to live outside of confinement and it was glorious. There was no intellectual explanation or scientific theory for it. It was just a feeling—a feeling that could only be enjoyed in the moment it was experienced. It was pure love and couldn't be overshadowed by other perceptions. Fear, hate, sadness, and pain were transformed.

His heart was beating wildly as the anxiety over everything that had happened to him in Eve flooded back in. He still had butterflies about what his trip to Friday Harbor would bring. In so many ways he was making large strides in his life, yet he still didn't feel free to choose the way he wanted his life to be.

He traveled down the stairway, hoping that finally he might have a normal day, a fun day at a festival, accompanied by a very attractive woman. He prayed to God not to let anything happen to him today.

He could see the outline of people through the stained glass windows in the front doors as he passed through the foyer. He could hear laughter as he got closer. For the time being it put him at ease. He walked out the front door and was bathed in sunlight. It was so warm and refreshing after having spent the previous day in a dark jail cell. It was another reason to be thankful, which calmed him further.

He looked at the four woman standing on the porch talking and laughing. By the tone of the lighthearted conversation they were engaged in, life appeared quite pleasant.

Adam smiled. "Good morning, ladies. It sure is a beautiful day."

The women were as giddy as schoolgirls. He represented a diversion and a source of hope that a better way of life was in fact possible.

Adam had interpreted the behavior of all the First Baptist's parishioners simply as warm, Christian charity. He really didn't have a clue about the impact his presence was having. Most of his life he had been exposed to black Baptists. His father was a deacon in a church in Detroit, so he would sometimes oblige him by attending a service. The people were always receptive and friendly. He didn't see beyond this to understand he represented the possibility for a new identity, in a small, southern town whose black population, up until now, had only seen themselves through a lens of blatant oppression.

"Well, I guess I'm ready for the festivities," he said as he walked up and joined Teri.

"I don't know if a city boy like yourself can handle the amount of fun that's in store for you today," she replied. "Are you sure you can handle this?"

The group chuckled and Teri introduced him to everyone.

"Well, the parade is set to start in about twenty minutes," she said. "We had better get going. We don't want to miss the church's float. Mrs. Jacobson and the children worked so hard on it."

With that said they walked together toward Town Square to watch the day's events. Along the way Adam was barraged with a plethora of questions about flying and related subjects, which he politely answered. He was also asked several probing questions about his personal life. The focus invariably was his marital status and what plans he had to change that.

"Mr Freeman, are you married?" Mrs Johnson asked.

"You know Adam, Teri here is probably the smartest and prettiest girl in Eve. She's gonna' be a lawyer soon," one of the other ladies said.

"It will be a lucky man that catches her fancy," another added.

They were both embarrassed by such personal inquiries, Teri less so than Adam. To some degree she was thankful for the assistance she was receiving from her elders, since she seemed more than happy to engage in a relationship with Adam.

When they arrived at Main Street, the parade was just getting underway. The street was lined on both sides with onlookers. The sounds of marching bands could be heard from everywhere along the route. Children's faces were filled with the magic that only such a spectacle could elicit. It really was a special sight to behold.

In spite of all the town's ills, this one event seemed to pull everyone together. Although the street was still divided according to race—the whites on the west side and the blacks on the east—there were a few of each group on the other's side. It seemed to be more for convenience than intended to make any kind of a statement and was let slide without conflict. Everyone just went on enjoying the event. As the head of the parade reached the end of the street, Adam noticed all of the blacks' floats turning right and all of the whites' turning left. He asked Teri about it and she explained about the two concurrently running festival picnics. She said it had been like that for years, at least as long as she could remember.

Adam just shook his head, reminded this was not the place he intended to stay. It would only be a matter of hours before he could get back on track to the place he felt he should be spending this part of his life. He felt grateful he wasn't going to be stuck here, like so many seemed to be.

He looked down at Teri. "Teri, how can you stand it?"

She looked back at him. "I can't, but I was born and raised here and this is my home. This town hasn't changed much in the twenty-three years I've seen. That's why I chose to study law. I'll make a difference in the courts. I sent my entrance application to Georgetown University a while back. Hopefully, I'll be hearing if they've accepted me."

Adam, mildly surprised, muttered, "Law, hmm. Now that's impressive. Well, good luck. I hope you get in. If you do, I'll fly you there personally."

"I'd like that," she replied, as they continued watching the procession streaming down Main Street.

It was such a strange experience watching the parade and listening to the crowd's reaction. Because the floats were alternating between white and black as they came down the route, you would hear loud cheers from one side and virtual silence on the other as each group lent support to only their race's floats. A black float got wild cheers from the east side of the street, a white float got cheers from the west side. It didn't seem as if anyone but Adam noticed this phenomenon.

He reasoned that after generations of living in a separatist society, they had become desensitized to it. Events as blatant as this to an outsider didn't even draw the slightest response from most of Eve's citizens, and it continued like this throughout the entire parade.

Soon there was a loud cheering from everyone on the street. It seemed that someone very popular was approaching. Adam nudged closer to get a better look, and as he did, he found himself firmly nudged up against the back of Teri. For a moment he really didn't notice how firmly he was pressed up against her derriere. When he became aware of it, he looked down at her in embarrassment and quickly backed away.

"Oh my God, I'm sorry. I didn't mean—"

"It's fine," she said smiling. "Don't worry about it."

She reached back and grabbed his hands and wrapped them around her waist. He wondered what the heck was going on.

It's not that he minded. It was just that romance seemed to move along pretty quickly in these parts. He also wasn't convinced this romance was exactly what he needed to be participating in right now.

He stood there behind Teri with his hands wrapped around her waist. As good as the warm softness of her body felt to him, he couldn't shake the awkwardness he felt being in this position so quickly. He continued to hold her as the wild cheering of the crowd got closer to where they were standing.

He had a pretty good vantage point of the paraders passing by. Now the cheers were right on top of him. He looked to see who it was. Coming down the route was a float decorated like a forest. On it was a group of small children dressed up to look like assorted wildflowers. Adam recognized some of the kids from the day he had spoken at the school. He also noticed a woman on the float dressed up as a gardener. He took a closer look at the woman who was smiling and waving at the crowd in both directions. She seemed familiar.

He was stunned and let go of Teri's waist as he inched a little closer to the street. His facial expression was like that of a small child gazing longingly at a puppy through a glass window, a puppy he knew he would never have. She turned and looked in his direction and their eyes met. She, too, was stunned. Marlena stopped waving and just stood there for a moment as she rode along on the float.

She gave Adam a half smile and then returned to her parade routine of smiling and waving to the crowd. As the float passed, still the cheers grew louder. Adam was in a daze, almost forgetting where he was and why.

Teri, noticing his hypnotic state, nudged him with her elbow. "You all right up there?" she asked affectionately as she looked up at him.

"Yeah. Yeah, I'm fine, thanks. I just remembered something I have to do."

As the crowd roared around him, he glanced back at the float and asked Teri, "Why such a response for the children's float?"

Teri lightly chuckled. "That's not for the children." She turned and pointed at the next float coming down the route. "That, is why this crowd is going so wild."

Adam looked at the float. It was decorated in a football motif, with goalposts, red jerseys, helmets, black cleats, and the team mascot, a reddish-brown bulldog. Alongside the float was strung a large banner that read: 1978 LOUISIANA STATE CHAMPS—EVE HIGH BULLDOGS.

"That is the only Eve High School team to achieve anything. Seven years later and the town is still celebrating. Every year, they have that float in the parade, with Brad there out in front."

Adam took a closer look at the man. He recognized him as the same guy Marlena was talking to outside the cafe a couple of days ago. With hidden contempt for the man, Adam asked, "So, who exactly is Brad?"

"Brad was the team's all-American quarterback. Most believe he was the sole reason for the team's success. He was supposed to wind up being a big-time college player at LSU, but I think he tore up his knees and ended up dropping out of school. Now he runs his dad's maintenance company in town. Everyone in Eve loves him. It's like he gave people in town a positive identity. On the other hand, no one speaks much of Isiah."

She pointed to a very large black man, also riding on the float. He was standing at the very back. Isiah was at least six-foot three, two hundred and fifty pounds with virtually no body-fat. He had a deep brown complexion, the color of dark swiss chocolate.

"Isiah played both fullback and linebacker positions. He led the team in rushing yards, tackles, and sacks. He was also an all- American, but never got recruited because of his grades. Isiah is a little slow. Back then no one took the time to tutor or help him along. They just kind of passed him through so he could help the team win ballgames. When he graduated, he couldn't even read a college application to fill it out. So he never made it any further than Eve. He's kind of a flunky boy for anyone who needs some heavy work done. It's really sort of pitiful."

"Man, that's too bad," Adam said, sympathizing with Isiah's circumstances.

"Yeah, but it's getting a little better. Brad has given Isiah a steady job with his dad's company. Also, your friend the schoolteacher started tutoring him a night or two a week when she found out he couldn't read. I guess he's making some progress. If I were you, I wouldn't get my hopes up too high on her. I think the whole town already has her and Brad matched up for life. That's why they've put their floats one after the other in the parade the last few years. It's kind of funny to watch."

Adam was taken aback by her comment and responded abruptly, "What do mean, get my hopes up?"

"I saw the way you looked at her that day in the cafe. And here again, today. There is definitely something going on. But in this town, it just ain't gonna happen. Don't worry, though, I'll make you forget you ever met her."

She smiled warmly at him, then grabbed him around his waist and hugged him. All around them the crowd was going crazy as Brad began throwing small nerf footballs into the crowd. Adam just stood there holding Teri as he watched Marlena's float move down the route and out of sight.

28.

The air was filled with the sweet smell of meat cooking on huge barrel grills. There were ribs, chicken, spicy smoked sausage, catfish, and what seemed to be an endless supply of fresh corn. At the long table, a veritable feast of accompaniments included coleslaw, baked beans, macaroni and cheese, collard greens, black-eyed peas laced with ham hocks and fatback, cornbread, rolls, fresh salad, and more. The desserts were as plentiful as they were decadent, and everything was homemade—chocolate cakes, sweet potato, apple, and cherry pies. There were deep pans full of peach cobbler. It was an incredible display of southern culinary excellence.

Adam was overwhelmed by the amount of food. At every turn, someone was encouraging him to eat more—as much and as often as he liked.

"There's plenty," they would say, as if somehow he might not have noticed. He realized they were simply displaying their southern hospitality, and it impressed him greatly.

Everyone had shed their Sunday church clothes for T-shirts, cutoff shorts, and other more comfortable picnic wear. Children were running around everywhere. Some played organized activities and games, others just ran about wildly, having the time of their lives. The adults were sitting around several large, round tables set up throughout the park. They were discussing today's church service and other issues of concern. Although engaged, they were always cognizant of the children's activities around them. A parent's occasional "Be careful" or "Share with your sister" could be heard.

Adam and Teri were invited to sit at the table with Reverend Jacobson's family and some of the church deacons and their relatives. Much of the afternoon, Adam fielded questions about his background and a myriad of inquiries about his flying and the crash.

Everyone was fascinated by his piloting exploits and his plans to buy an airport. It was as if he were some kind of celebrity who had just dropped in to pay the town an impromptu visit. Throughout the day, people stopped over at the table to make his acquaintance and wish him well. For the most part, Teri sat beside him feeling the pride of being his escort, at least for the day.

When the stream of well-wishers finally slowed, Adam turned to Teri. "So, tell me more about your plans for law school."

She smiled. "Well, don't I feel special. I thought you were answering all the questions today." She smiled again and held his hand to reassure him that she meant no harm.

"Well, like I told you, I hope to hear from Georgetown University fairly soon. I'm pretty confident I'll get in. I've carried a three-point-eight GPA ever since I started junior college. I have also applied for an internship with a congressman—Blaise Douglass—at his office in D.C. So, hopefully, I can earn some money while I'm attending school. I hope it all works out, but in this world you never know. I'm prepared for whatever happens."

"Well, I'm sure things will work out for the best. You're an awfully bright young woman."

"Well, thank you, Adam. That means a lot to me coming from you. And don't forget you owe me a ride to Washington when it happens."

They looked at each other with a sense of genuine kinship. At that moment, a large man approached the table. He reached out his hand to Adam.

"Hi, I'm Isiah. It's a pleasure to make your acquaintance, Mr. Freeman."

Not only was Isiah's drawl quite heavy, but his speech was also slow. It was as if he deliberately slowed his speech to make sure he didn't make a mistake, say the wrong thing, and embarrass himself.

"I've heard a whole lot about you, Mr. Freeman."

"Adam—call me Adam, Isiah. I've heard a lot of good things about you as well. Word is that you were a pretty good ball player. No, I'm sorry, I mean a great ball player. 1978, huh? I think that I remember you."

"You do?" Isiah responded incredulously. "You ain't even from around here."

"You were an all-American, right?"

"Well, yeah, but—"

"I was on that same all-American team. I was just a junior and only got an honorable mention, but I was selected best of the Northwest. I vaguely recall reading about a big, bruisin' boy from down south that played fullback and linebacker. Although the details are fuzzy, I do remember you. They say you led Eve to the title."

Isiah smiled bashfully "Well, you know ol' Brad was a heck of a quarterback. He probably had more to do with it than I did. What position did you play?"

"I was a wide receiver and defensive back."

"So, you were a football hero, too." Teri said to Adam. "I am impressed. I don't know why that surprises me. You've probably been successful your whole life."

"As a matter of fact, Ms. Jones, there was a period in my life where I believed myself to be a miserable failure, and I was. I had just barely enough credits to graduate from high school. I had to take an English class at night school during my final semester in order to graduate on time. No, I guess I'm more of a testament to how someone can turn their life around, which it's never too late to do. Right, Isiah?"

He glanced over at Isiah and the two men smiled at each other. Adam then asked Isiah how he was at working with his hands and if he had ever considered working on airplanes. He told him about some mechanic training centers he knew of and scribbled their names down on a piece of paper. He also referred him to the financial aid program he had used to fund his flight training. As Adam was finishing, he heard someone calling to Isiah.

"Well, I guess I better go see what my wife wants," Isiah said. "It was nice to meet you. Maybe I'll see ya'll later." With that he turned and began to walk away.

Adam yelled after him, "If you decide to become a aero-mechanic, be sure and look me up in Friday Harbor. I might just have a job for you."

Isiah turned back and smiled, waving one arm in acknowledgment of Adam's generous gesture.

Reverend Jacobson returned to the table from making his rounds, offering blessings to all the picnickers.

"Whew! This is hard work," he said, as he plopped down in his seat.

"Reverend Jacobson, this is supposed to be a fun day. Can't the Lord give you the day off?" said one of his party jokingly.

Everyone chuckled and continued their conversations.

Reverend Jacobson leaned across the table to Adam. "Adam, I understand you'll probably be in town for a couple more days. I want you to know you are more than welcome to stay with me and the Mrs. or, if you desire, you can keep your current accommodations at the church. It's entirely up to you."

"Well, thank you, Reverend Jacobson. That's quite kind. I'm sure I'll take you up on one of those offers. I'm just not sure which one right now. Thank you very much."

As the day drew to a close, the sun was falling behind the surrounding trees. It blessed the evening sky with brilliant hues of orange and magenta. Birds and crickets could be heard off in the distance accompanying nature's dance with songs of their own. Many stood for a moment of silence, just taking it all in and giving thanks. It had been a long afternoon, and although several were ready to call it a day, there was more to come. It just wouldn't be a proper conclusion to the Blossom Festival without staying for the annual fireworks. Some of the elders napped where they sat, while the youth seemed to gear up, fueled by their excitement over the coming pyrotechnics.

Teri reached over and held Adam's hand as she noticed him gazing off in quiet reflection. She leaned over and whispered, "Come on, let's take a walk. You look like you're going to suffer the same fate as elder Jonathan." She motioned towards Jonathan, who was asleep in his chair, slouched over with his head bobbing back and forth.

Adam laughed at Teri's remark and nodded. They excused themselves and got up from the table. Teri led Adam to the east fork of the stream that ran through town.

"Adam, have you ever gotten a job through affirmative action?" Teri asked.

"No, Teri, I haven't." Adam answered. "Why?"

"Well, what do you think of it?" She asked.

"I don't know for sure," he answered. "But in alot of cases I think that it can be pretty damaging. I mean do you think that Michael Jordan is in the NBA, and perhaps the greatest player of all-time because someone had to meet a quota—no. He is that because he has taken his God given talent and worked on it incessantly until he became what he is. If—"

"Adam, the people in this town aren't Michael Jordan." Teri interjected. "If not for program's like it, most people in this town would have no shot at all. I know I wouldn't. You think you're

so—"

"Teri, I'm sorry. I don't mean to sound like I don't care about people who have less opportunity, especially you. I think it's obvious how brilliant you are, and I am in no way trying to make light any of your accomplishments. I just don't like the idea of an entire race of people believing that the only way that they can acheive and make the most of themselves is if the establishment reserves them a place or gives them a head start. I believe that we are more than capable of exploding on whichever scene we chose by our own devices, hard work and God given talents."

"Adam, that sounds very utopic. The fact is, our people need these programs because of how far behind this establishment has put us in the first place. As wonderful as what you said was, it is harder for us to get over than it is for them. That has got to change."

"I understand, Teri. I understand." Adam said as he looked toward the sky. "What we have been through as a people, gives us more character, courage and strength than the average person in our society could imagine. That alone gives us an edge, if we chose to see it that way, and draw upon it."

Teri stood silently for a moment, staring off at the trees in the distance. "You really are an incredible man Adam. You, are definately different from most," she said.

"You too, Teri. You are something special. I'm sure someday this town will name a street after you."

They smiled at each other and held hands, squeezing them as a confirmation of their feelings. The sky had now turned a fiery, reddish orange. It was dusk's visual song, trumpeting the coming of darkness. They took a seat on a soft, grassy clearing and just listened to the river's rushing melody.

29.

Lance sat behind the sheriff's desk reading the current *Sports Illustrated*. He heard a clank coming from outside. At first he paid no attention to it. Then he heard it again. As he walked toward the front door, a buxom young woman, obviously frazzled, burst into the sheriff's office.

Lance recognized the woman as Trisy, one of the locals who was known by most of Eve's male population because of her sexually alluring looks. Tall and pretty was she— her creamy white face centered by a small, almost perfectly straight nose. Crystal blue eyes assisted her in melting the heart of even the most resisting of souls. Trisy's dusty blonde hair was pulled back into a long ponytail reaching half way down her back. Her long shapely legs adorned by a pair of cutoff jeans, that just barely covered her taut round bottom. As Lance glanced at her, he could not help noticing her large breast spilling out of her bright yellow cropped top. As Trisy approached Lance, she looked around the room.

"Lance, is the sheriff here?" she asked in a thick, southern drawl.

"No, he's not," he answered curtly. "Is there something I can help you with?"

"Oh darn! Well, I just got a flat tire down the road and there ain't no one around to help me. Sheriff and Clint usually help me when I have a problem with my car, but I can't find them anywhere."

She moved closer to Lance, seductively pressing her heaving breasts up against him. "Please, Lance. It won't take long. You don't know just how much I would appreciate it if ya helped me."

She knew just how to look at Lance to make him succumb. Lance smelled a reward in all of this, one he couldn't pass up. He looked down at Trisy's cleavage, which was very apparent underneath the low-cut top she had on, and answered, "Well sure, Trisy. I have a prisoner here, so I'll have to lock the place up. You just wait outside and I'll be right out."

Trisy thanked him and did as he suggested. He quickly straightened up the magazines and papers he had scattered about the sheriff's desk throughout the day. He also wrote a quick note, just in case the sheriff came back before he did.

Lance had peeked in on Clint and found him sound asleep. He double-locked the door to the cell block and exited out the front of the building. He began whistling a happy tune, looking forward to helping this damsel in distress and reaping his reward. When he got out onto the porch, he didn't see her anywhere.

"Trisy. Trisy, are you there?"

There was no sign of her. He began walking toward the steps when he felt a sharp pain in back of his head. He fell to the ground, and everything went black.

Big Jim was standing over Lance holding the night stick. He turned to Zak and said nervously, "You got the rope, right?"

"Yeah, I got the rope, ya oaf," Zak replied.

Trisy came from behind the shrubs around the front of the sheriff's building and cheerily asked, "How'd I do, guys?"

Zak turned to her as he and Big Jim tied Lance up.

"You did great. Now get the hell out of here. We'll see you later on."

Trisy, perturbed by his rudeness, shot back, "But what about my money?"

"I said, we'll see you later," Zak replied. "Now get the hell out of here. Now!"

Trisy scurried away.

When Lance's hands and feet were tied, he began to come to. He started grumbling, "What the...what happened?"

"Lance, you hit your head and you're delirious," Zak said. "Here, take this." Zak forced a tranquilizer down his throat and in a few minutes, Lance was out cold.

They searched through his pockets and found his keys, then they picked him up, took him over to his squad car, and put him in the trunk. Jim got into the car and pulled it to the back of the building. He and Zak found the key to the back door and opened it. then made their way up front to the entrance of the cell block, They unlocked the cell block doors. "Clint, yo! Clint where ya at?"

"Hey, guys, over here," The answer came from the back. "What the hell took you so long? Sheriff's not gonna be gone all goddamn night, you know."

"Sorry, Clint. It took awhile to convince Trisy to go along with it. We finally had to promise her money, a lot of it."

Jim unlocked the cell door and the three men made their way out the back of the building. They all piled into the brown pickup that was parked in the alley and sped off.

"You boys got the stuff?" Clint said.

Sitting in the rear of the cab, Jim reached down and grabbed a high-powered, bolt-action rifle and proudly held it up for Clint's inspection. He pulled the spring-action bolt back and it made a loud clink. It was loaded and ready to go.

"Where's the sheriff?" Clint asked in a pleased voice.

Zak timidly answered, "We still don't know. We had him up until about an hour ago, then we lost him."

"Goddamn it!" Clint responded. "Well, where's the nigger?"

Zak, this time more assured, answered, "With the rest of them at the picnic."

"Well, let's do it then!" Clint said. They all smiled devilishly.

Zak held up a bottle of Tennessee whiskey and took a big swig as the men all yelped, speeding down the road on the way to take care of business.

30.

Teri and Adam sat on the bank of the stream talking. Through the course of their conversation they had unknowingly moved very close together. Teri looked into Adam's big brown eyes and said, "Adam, I don't often find men that are anything like you, especially around here. I mean, you are accomplished in a highly respected and exciting profession, yet you are so down-to-earth. How do you do it?"

Adam smiled, pleased with the compliment. "Well, I don't know. I guess I've always been this way. I don't feel like I've done anything that anyone else couldn't do, given the right opportunity. I guess I just feel thankful to be in the position I'm in. If there's anything I would like to be different, it's that I wish I had more time to help others, the way a man once helped me."

"I'm sure at some point, when the time is right, you will," she said. "You have a really good heart. That's one of the things that I like about you." She drew her face closer as she leaned over to kiss him. First on the cheek, then she reached her hand up and cupped his face as she closed her eyes and kissed him on the lips. Adam's eyes widened in disbelief. He relaxed into the kiss and closed his eyes. Seconds later, he quickly pulled away and stood up.

"What's wrong? Did I do something wrong?" Teri asked.

Adam stood there shaking his head. "No. No, you didn't do anything wrong. You were just doing what people do. I was the one who did something wrong. I shouldn't be doing this. Teri, I think you are a wonderful, young woman. You are incredibly beautiful, you're bright. In any other circumstance I would be all over you, but you gotta know my heart is just somewhere else right now. I just can't do this. It's not fair to either one of us. I'm sorry. I need to go sort this out. Why don't I walk you back to the table?"

Teri sighed in disappointment. Pouting, she rolled her eyes at him, silently stood up and followed him back to the picnic area.

The excitement in the air was building, as the children anticipated the fireworks display that was now less than an hour away. Adam and Teri arrived back at the table to find Reverend Jacobson and the deacons caught up in a rousing theological debate. They were so enthralled that they barely noticed Adam's and Teri's return. Teri sat down and quickly picked up a conversation with one of the elder women. She did a good job of disguising her hurt feelings.

Adam quickly excused himself, saying he needed to go find a bathroom. He really just wanted to walk to a quiet spot to gather his thoughts and clear his mind.

Reverend Jacobson, noticing Adam's departure, yelled over to him, "Don't get lost, son. You're about to witness some of the finest fireworks that this country has to offer."

He smiled and waved at Adam, then picked up exactly where he had left off in the debate. Adam wandered off toward the trees he saw in the distance. It looked quiet over there and no one else was in sight. It seemed the perfect place to find some peace. Drawing nearer to the forest, he noticed it went back a significant distance. He succumbed to his spirit of adventure and headed into the large maple and walnut trees.

As he walked, his mind drifted back to the crash and he pondered the reason for his being brought to this place. He had read somewhere that everything in life happened for a reason. He wondered what in hell could have been the purpose behind this dreadful experience. His mind went to the stunningly beautiful Marlena Thompson and his heart quivered. He couldn't remember ever falling so hard for a woman.

He recalled the first sight of her in the clinic and how beautiful she looked—the way her dress fell so perfectly over her sculpted form. Again, he experienced the rush he got when she first smiled at him. It was disheartening for him to think he would never see her again, never again kiss her or feel the warmth of her skin pressed against his, or smell the sweet fragrance of her perfume.

Nightfall was upon Eve and Adam had to focus on the ground to find his way. It was almost time for the fireworks. He resolved that he just needed to get over it—to never see her again was what was truly best. Maybe all of this had happened so that God could illustrate just how wonderful love could feel when you found that special someone.

Adam headed back toward the picnic grounds, but after walking for a few minutes he noticed he was going in circles. He was lost. He began to feel bad that he was going to miss the beginning of the fireworks. He knew how much everyone wanted to share the experience with him. It was an event they were all very proud of.

He decided to head in a different direction, in search of some recognizable landmark. For a moment, he thought he saw something that looked familiar, but realized he was hopelessly lost. Suddenly, he saw some lights ahead and began to walk briskly towards them. As he got closer, he could see it was the flurry of activity at the picnic grounds.

He was about a quarter of a mile away when he saw people congregating. They were all walking in the same direction. He figured they must be gathering for the festival fireworks. He was just in time.

When he reached the clearing, he began to feel a little displaced. He continued to walk toward the throng of people moving in the direction of Johnston's Point to view the fireworks. As he got closer, he noticed that all of these people were white.

"Oh, shit!" he exclaimed out loud. "I've wandered over to the wrong picnic. This is the last place that I need to be. Shit!"

He looked at the people and then back at the forest. He scanned the outer row of trees, trying to figure the best way to get back. He wondered how in the world he'd gotten over here. Again, he observed the exodus of people, which was clearing the area fairly quickly. He thought that maybe he could wait until the grounds cleared completely, make a dash for the street, and work his way back down Main.

He saw two people still standing next to their table. It appeared they were deep in conversation. As he looked at them, he recognized the woman's silhouette. He moved a little closer to get a better look. It was her. It was Marlena.

She was standing across from Eve's football hero, Brad. Jealousy overtook him once again. He saddened as he watched the two of them talking. At one point, Marlena leaned forward and hugged Brad. As they held their embrace, Adam's heart bled. As much as it hurt, this crushing blow was exactly what he needed to be able to bring closure to these circumstances and to move on with his life.

He stood there watching for a few seconds longer, devastated. He turned toward the forest from which he had just come, and deliberately walked away.

"Adam?" Marlena called out after him.

She began to move faster as she pursued him. She turned to Brad and explained, "Brad, I need to go sort something out. I'll catch up, okay!"

Brad nodded and watched her as she took off after Adam.

"Adam!" she called again, her pace quickening.

He was now in the forest, wading among the trees, out of her line of sight.

Adam kept walking further into the woods, not knowing exactly where he was going. He just wanted to get as far away as possible. He couldn't hide his hurt and he wanted no part of trying to express his feelings. Marlena continued her pursuit, now only fifty or so yards behind him. She could see him trying to escape through the majestic trees, pretending not to hear her. Finally, she was close enough that ignoring her was futile.

"Adam!" she forcefully called out. "You can't pretend you don't hear me. Unless, of course, you have recently been in an awful accident and lost your hearing." She smiled.

Adam stopped, his back to her. He was glad she couldn't see he was amused by her comment. They both stood silently, she behind him, looking at his back and waiting for a response.

In an attempt to keep things light, he said, "Well, as a matter of fact, I was recently in an awful accident. I lost my hearing, I can't see very well, and I also broke my heart in two places. You see, I found myself lost in these woods until I happened upon a clearing. I thought I had found my way back to the First Baptist Blossom Day picnic, until I saw a mirage. I really thought I had regained my vision, but then realized I must be imagining seeing someone I used to know all hugged up with the town's former football hero."

He turned around, the pain evident on his face. "I guess you go for former high school football greats." He tightened his lips and fought back the urge to express his anger further. There was no way on earth she would see his true feelings, not under these circumstances.

She looked at the ground as she thought for a moment. Her anguish was clearly evident as she searched for the right words. She looked at him. "I thought you didn't want to have anything to do with me."

"So you went running back to Joe Montana? I guess you got over me pretty quick, huh? I don't know what I expected. You were over me in about the same amount of time it took you to fall for me. Hey listen, I'm sorry. I'm out of place here. I only ended up here because I got lost in these woods. What I saw was none of my business. You were right, I told you that we shouldn't see each other and—"

Adam was startled by the loud explosions that seemed to come out of nowhere. The sky lit up as the Blossom Day fireworks began.

"Whew!" he exclaimed. "What a shock." He grabbed his chest.

Marlena was standing in front of him, smiling at the whole scene.

He began to laugh. "Wow, was that loud. I thought a bomb had just gone off or something. Woo, boy. Now, where was I? Oh yeah..."

He fixed a serious scowl on his face as he remembered where the discussion was headed. "I was just explaining to you that—"

"You were just going to tell me that you hate me. You were going to say that you never did love me and the best thing for you to do was to get as far away from me as fast as possible. Right?"

As they stood there talking, the loud explosions and illuminations from the fireworks were lighting up the sky.

"Well, I wasn't exactly going to put it that—"

"Go ahead," she said. "Look me in my eye and tell me you don't love me and that you don't want anything else to do with me."

They stood no more than two feet apart, looking intently into each other's eyes. Adam was speechless and finally had to look away, for the more he gazed into her eyes the more he was drawn back into his passion for her.

"By the way," she continued, "what you saw was nothing more than a friendly hug—a thank you for all of the work that Brad did helping the kids prepare for the parade. You think I'm over you, Adam Freeman? I don't think so. I will take the way you look at me to my grave. I fall into a place that feels like heaven on earth every time we look into each other's eyes. No one has ever had that effect on me."

Again, they looked into each other's eyes. All of their emotions returned and for the moment all guards were down. The joy they first experienced with one another filled their hearts.

Marlena, looking deeply into Adam's soul, said, "Tell me that you don't love me."

There was a silence as Adam turned away.

Again they were startled by an explosion that seemed even stronger than the previous ones. He looked up to the sky, briefly admiring the impressive display, then looked back into Marlena's eyes. She stood there solemnly awaiting his response.

Very slowly he started to speak, his tone a bit remorseful. "Marlena, I don't..." he moved his face closer to hers as she waited in quiet anticipation. "...ever want to be without you."

The tears welled up in her eyes as he finished. The last thing he saw before their lips met was a single tear rolling down her cheek. They clenched each other in an embrace that seemed a thousand years coming. As they kissed, the fireworks lit up the night sky all around them. As they held each other, their desire grew.

Marlena experienced a tingle throughout her body and squeezed him tighter, pressing every part of her body against his. Adam increased his grip and found himself caressing her back just above her soft derriere. The suppleness of her skin underneath and the smooth feel of her thin, rayon sundress urged him on. He reached down and squeezed her curvaceous buttocks, pulling her even closer.

She let out a sigh, "Oh, Adam!"

His nervousness about what he was doing quickly gave way to desire. His hands slowly explored all up and down the back of her body as they continued their kiss. She began to respond in kind, grabbing his firm behind. She held it with both hands, squeezing his body firmly against hers. They began letting out occasional sighs and moans of pleasure. His hands slid up to her shoulders and he gently massaged them, moving his hands up around her neck and caressing her face.

The passion between them escalated as the loud explosions from the fireworks were going off overhead. Marlena rubbed his chest until she could no longer stand feeling the material that covered his caramel-brown skin. She reached up and unbuttoned the top three buttons of his shirt and slid her hands inside to feel the bare nakedness of his flesh. He was warm, and her fingertips found his now erect nipples. She fondled them, further fueling his already heightened desire.

Adam continued massaging her arms and shoulders. He caressed her face as she slid her hand down inside his shirt to his stomach. She could feel how tight his stomach muscles were and she sighed in delight. He was becoming increasingly aroused the more she explored him.

Any hesitations he had were now gone as he reached down and slid his hand up the front of her dress. He gently stroked her well-shaped thighs. She slid her hand down and felt the firmness in his pants. He moved his hand up the inside of her thighs and cupped his hand between her legs, feeling the moist warmth there. They continued to touch each other intimately, now completely consumed.

Surrendering themselves to their desires, they slid down onto the ground. Laying there on a bed of leaves, they were oblivious to the world around them. Their bodies ached for one another, but a moment as special as this couldn't possibly be rushed. They kissed, fondled, and gave pleasure to one another until finally neither one could stand it any longer.

"Adam, I want you!"

Adam, kissing Marlena's neck and slowly working his way down her now unbuttoned shirt, responded, "Yes."

As he kissed and caressed her beautiful breast, she begged him, "Adam, please. I want you—now. Come to me."

Adam rolled on top her and looked at her lovely face. He was lost in spiritual ecstasy, as he fell deeply into her eyes. She reached up and put her arms around him, then rubbed his arms. He moved even closer to her, feeling the warmth flowing from inside her.

Adam suddenly felt a sharp pain in his back, and rolled off Marlena, writhing and groaning in pain.

There above Adam stood Zak and Big Jim. Jim was holding a baseball bat, the one he had just used to bash Adam across the back. Zak looked down at Marlena, who had scrambled over to assist Adam.

"Well, well, well, look what we have here," Zak said. "It looks like we just saved this fair lady from bein' raped by this nigger. Huh, Jimmy?"

Jim nodded.

Zak then turned toward Marlena and asked with a bit of sarcasm, "Pardon me, ma'am. Can we be of any further assistance to you in this, your moment of need? I mean you looked to be a bit worked up. Maybe you need a couple of real men to put out yer fire." As he finished his statement, he began to move closer to her.

Marlena snapped, "Don't even think about it! Do you see what you have done? You could've killed him, you assholes."

Zak just kept moving toward her. He began to pull down his zipper and violently grabbed her.

"No!" she screamed as he lunged forward.

"Ow, goddamn it!" Zak screamed.

Adam had leapt from the ground with a handful of dirt and threw it in Zak's eyes. Zak clutched his face.

Adam kneed Zak in the gut and as he bent over in pain, Adam elbowed his neck, sending him flailing to the ground. Big Jim wound up to give Adam another shot with the Louisville slugger.

Again, Jim's bat found its mark and sent Adam crashing to the ground. Zak slowly and groggily got up from the ground, swearing at Adam and his attempted heroics.

"Goddamn nigger, you're gonna pay for that," Zak said. "First we're gonna let you watch us do this bitch. Then, we're gonna let her watch us kill you."

Adam screamed as Zak kicked him in the gut.

"Come here, bitch," Zak yelled as Marlena began to cry.

As he approached her, Jim gave Adam another kick in the gut to ensure that he had no further heroics left in him. Then Jim walked over to where Zak was stalking Marlena, as she pleaded for mercy. Jim came up from behind and grabbed her arms to keep her still. She could feel sweat dripping down from his face, falling onto her forehead. Both men stank, as if they hadn't bathed for a few days. The thought of what they were about to do to her made her nauseous, and she was terrified.

She began to wiggle wildly, trying to break free of the grasp of the strapping, six foot five, 260-pound man everyone referred to as "Big" Jim. Zak had him lay her down on the ground in front of him while he unzipped his pants and prepared to force himself on her. Her legs kicked and her body twisted, but finally he got a hold of her and spread her legs. He moved himself between her legs and began to smile.

"Now, little honey this ain't gonna hurt a—"

Zak fell forward and his head landed right in Marlena's bosom. He lay there limp, his full weight dead on top of her. Jim and Marlena both looked over to where Adam was laying and to their surprise he was still there, groaning in pain. They looked around and there stood Brad, bat in hand. He had it cocked back behind his head, taking steady aim directly at Jim.

The bat went crashing into Jim's head and he immediately went limp, falling back onto the ground. Marlena moved Zak off from on top of her and then held her head in her hands. She was exhausted—physically and emotionally. Her dress was covered with blood from Zak's head. Brad had hit both men in the head and for all she knew they were both dead. Brad walked over to the men, only a few feet from one another, laying motionless on the ground. He reached down and checked their necks for pulses. They weren't dead, but from what he could feel, their pulses were pretty faint.

Brad went over to Marlena, who was kneeling on the ground, bent over sobbing with her head in her hands. He reached down and lifted her up, holding her gently in his arms. He softly stroked her head and whispered to her, "Now what has my little fireball gone and gotten into?"

As they stood there, Adam began to come to. He lay on the ground groaning and rubbing his head as he looked around the area, trying to gauge what was going on. He noticed the two men laying a few feet from him on the ground. Then, he saw Marlena and Brad embracing one another. "Well, if you are thanking him again, thank him for me too," he muttered.

Marlena smiled and looked over at Adam, who was struggling to stand up. She and Brad went over to give him a hand. When Adam got to his feet, Marlena embraced him. She held him tightly; she intended to give him the message that she never wanted to let him go. She leaned up and kissed him, a symbol that assured everyone present exactly where her affections lay.

She turned to Brad and introduced the two men. "Brad, I'd like you to meet a very special man, Adam Freeman. Adam, this is my dear friend and now lifesaver, Brad Stackhouse."

The two shook hands and Brad commented, "Well, Mr. Freeman, I've heard a lot of good things about you."

Adam smiled. "Brad, I've heard some good things about you as well."

Adam looked over at Marlena, and smiled slyly. She lowered her eyebrows quizzically, not knowing what to make of his comment.

Marlena, Adam, and Brad began gathering their belongings when Brad noticed some pieces of rope that Zak and Jim had brought with them. The rope was most likely intended for Adam's lynching. He picked it up, and decided to tie them up in case they came to before he could notify the sheriff.

As they prepared to leave the forest, they noticed the well- orchestrated chorus of lights and explosions taking place in the sky above them. It was the grand finale, and what a spectacle it was. They stood watching until the sky again became silent and dark, littered with brilliant stars. Brad turned and led the three of them back to where he and Marlena had been picnicking earlier.

The throngs of people that had been watching the fireworks were now making their way to their cars, oblivious to the events that had just taken place in the woods. No one seemed to even notice Adam, Marlena, and Brad sitting at a vacant picnic table.

Marlena told Brad how their ordeal had occurred. Brad, after getting the facts, went to call the sheriff at a pay phone about a half mile away. As Brad faded out of sight, Adam and Marlena looked at each other and both let out a deep sigh. What a night this had turned out to be.

Adam began to think about the possibility of having a relationship with this beautiful and passionate woman sitting across from him. He thought to himself, if they could survive this night, there couldn't be much else that could come between them. This week had to have been as bad as it gets. He smiled.

"I'm sorry, but smiling is about the last thing my face wants to do at the moment," Marlena said. "Can you explain to me what you're so happy about?"

Adam's mood was infectious and Marlena couldn't help but smile back at him.

"Well, I was just thinking, if everything we said before our rude interruption was true, then we have to figure out how this is going to work." He gazed into her eyes, his expression now turned to concern. "The problem, Marlena, is that I'm completely terrified of you. Wow, I have never said that to a woman before, but it's true. I ask myself, why me? What, if anything, do I have to offer to you?"

Marlena stood before him, absorbing every word.

"Marlena, yesterday you said that you realized you could love me, and that in fact you do love me. I just have a hard time with that—"

"Why?"

"Well, look at you. Look at where you come from and how you were raised. I couldn't imagine creating a home like the one you are used to, or being able to talk to you about art and museums and stuff like that." Adam finished in a somber tone, looking to her for a response.

"Adam, I'm not looking for a recreation of my upbringing. All I want is you and whatever is unique to that experience. I want who you are. I see the beauty in you and I couldn't possibly grow weary of it. To be quite honest, there are traits you have that I wish I had. I, however, am more than happy to enjoy them by simply being with you." She beamed at him.

Adam didn't quite know what to say. He just sat there for a moment taking it all in. "You mean you won't just make love with me once to satisfy your curiosity and then leave for someone that is more the type you want to settle down with?"

"Mr. Freeman, if tonight's session in the forest was any kind of a preview, I'd say there isn't a more suitable man for me, at least not on this planet. I think we will definitely be taking frequent walks in the woods," she said devilishly as she reached out, grabbed his hand, and looked longingly into his eyes.

"I guess things couldn't get any worse for us than what we've been through this past week. Everything after this should be cake." His face broke into a huge grin and Marlena mirrored it.

"Oh, Adam," she sighed, as she slid her body up next to his and wrapped her arms around him. "What am I going to do with you?"

"Marlena, whatever your heart desires. Whatever your little heart desires."

31.

Brad crossed Main Street and made his way back to the picnic table where he left Marlena and Adam sitting. As he approached them he stated, "Well, the sheriff's on his way here. I was able to reach him at his office. He didn't seem at all surprised when I told him what happened. It seems he'd been out looking for those two and Deputy Lake all night. He said they're up to something."

"They were up to something all right," Marlena responded.

"Sheriff Phillips seems to think it might be a good idea if you guys found a safe place to stay until he can locate Lake. I always knew he was a weasel."

Adam suggested they go over to the church and wait, but Marlena had another idea.

"Adam, let's just go to my parents' house. We'll be safe there. Mom and Dad were going straight home after the fireworks. Dad has a couple of hunting rifles, in case we need them. Come on, let's go there. My car is parked just down the road."

They all agreed that Marlena's suggestion was probably best.

"Why don't I walk you to your car." Brad said. "Then I'll go back and make sure those two are still restrained until Sheriff Phillips arrives."

They all gathered their belongings and began walking towards the car. Suddenly they heard a small voice yelling from a distance.

"Wait, Mrs. Thompson. Wait."

Running toward them and waving a piece of paper was little Ricky Mack. Although he was screaming as he frantically approached, they could see his wonderfully wide grin.

Marlena, Brad, and Adam all stood there smiling as he ran towards them. When he got close enough, he slowed his pace to a brisk walk. Even though he was winded he was still beaming. He again held up the sheet of paper in his right hand. He tried to speak, but his panting made his words difficult to understand. Adam reached down and put his hands on the boy's shoulders to calm him.

"It's okay, son. What is it you need to tell us?"

Ricky took a couple of deep breaths and tried again.

"I'm glad you guys are still here. I didn't know if I'd find you. When I couldn't find Mr. Freeman at the First Baptist picnic, I didn't know where else to look. I thought maybe he'd be with you, Miss Thompson."

Adam and Marlena looked at each other, both amused and puzzled.

"Is it that obvious?" Adam asked.

He looked over at Brad, who smiled and nodded.

Ricky held out the sheet of paper to Adam. As Adam accepted it, he could see it was one of Ricky's trademark drawings.

Adam studied the illustration of a man flying an airplane into a bright orange sunset.

For a child's drawing, it really was a wonderful depiction. Underneath the picture was written:

I hope your airplane gets fixed fast so you
can hurry up and come back again.

Adam was touched by the boy's gesture and impressed by his perceptiveness. Ricky seemed to completely understand Adam's need to go in search of his dream. This boy also seemed to know that, whether Adam liked it or not, he had a tie to this small town and all who were affected by his drive and faith. Adam had given them a glimpse of hope that, in fact, there was a better way to live.

Adam had become a beacon, a flicker of hope for the black citizenry of Eve. He was there, if for no other reason than to symbolize the importance of holding to one's dreams, even if they didn't appear to be immediately attainable.

Suddenly, shots rang out through the park, followed by a mournful scream. Marlena cried out in horror. Adam and Brad were momentarily frozen in shock as Ricky lay motionless on the ground, having unexpectedly jumped into Adam's arms just as the shots intended for Adam were fired.

The sheriff's car immediately appeared on the scene, screeching to a stop not far from where the group stood.

"Shit!" a voice exclaimed from the edge of the woods.

Brad looked in the direction he had just heard the expletive come from and he saw Clint reloading. He gritted his teeth in disgust. "No!" he yelled at the top of his voice.

He took off after Clint, who was standing in the shrubs, again taking aim at Adam. It was a moment that seemed to last forever. Brad was running full bore towards Clint, who was poised for the final kill. At the same time, Adam leapt over and pushed Marlena out of the way to ensure she wouldn't be the second innocent victim.

Sheriff Phillips, jumped out of the squad car and drew his pistol. He also began running at Clint, who was at this point a good sixty yards away. The sheriff took aim, steadying his arm holding the gun with his other hand, all the while running full stride toward his deputy.

"Clint!" he screamed.

Another shot rang out from Clint's rifle. Phillips saw Brad's body jerk and fall to the ground as he took the bullet.

Clint quickly pulled the bolt-action lever back and stood ready to shoot again.

"No!" Phillips screamed.

Phillips opened fire, still running directly at Clint and now only thirty yards away. All of the sheriff's shots missed as Clint again fired.

This time the bullet grazed Adam's left arm.

Phillips continued to fire, emptying his pistol and Clint tumbled to the ground. Clint was wounded, but was able to quickly gather himself and he started running into the forest.

Clint was moving slowly because of the bullet wounds he sustained. In the meantime, Brad got up and began trailing behind Sheriff Phillips. Clint left a trail of blood, having been hit at least twice by the sheriff's point-blank shots. Brad, too, was bleeding profusely from his right shoulder. He held it as he ran, trying to mentally overcome the pain. As Phillips and Brad entered the silent forest, there was no visible sign of Clint. They knew he couldn't have escaped that quickly, so they split in two directions to scout the area. Both got down on their hands and knees and crept through the forest as if in combat. Sheriff Phillips popped the empty clip out of his pistol and reloaded.

Shots whizzed by Phillips, but missed. Both Brad and Phillips looked to where the shots had originated from. They could barely make out a subtle movement behind one of the tall trees in the distance. Brad circled around to the right and the sheriff moved directly toward the rustling.

He took aim at the tree and fired a couple of shots. He could see the dark, shadowy figure move behind the tree for cover. He crept even closer, took aim, and fired again.

"Clint, I don't know what this is all about or how you got involved, but it's over. Give yourself up before things get any worse. I know you have some hateful beliefs about Negroes, but this has gone too far. Clint, you there? Clint!"

Phillips peered out from behind where he was taking cover.

Clint fired another shot.

"Okay, suit yourself then," Phillips responded.

Sheriff Phillips reached down and grabbed another clip from the belt for his holster and held it in his left hand as backup. He squared up with the tree protecting Clint from his view. At this point he was probably only twenty yards away and he opened fire.

He emptied his pistol and quickly reloaded. Clint got off one shot, but in an instant Phillips was spraying the tree with gunfire again.

Clint got off another shot, which was followed by a loud thud from the spot where he was hiding. Then the sheriff heard an ensuing scuffle. Brad had managed to sneak up behind Clint while he was distracted by the exchange of gunfire. Brad began pummeling the deputy with his fist, as the blood from his bullet wound streamed down his shoulder. He was so flooded with rage he was oblivious to his own affliction. Clint rallied and flipped Brad off of him, grabbing him by the throat. He punched Brad in the face and spat. "Goddamn nigger lover."

The two were wrestling on the ground as the sheriff reached the clearing. Again, Clint managed to pin Brad to the ground as he pulled a switchblade from where it was strapped just above his sock. He pushed the release button on the knife, and a seven-inch blade slid out of one end. He put the blade to Brad's throat and just as he was about to cut it, he heard another click.

Sheriff Phillips stood above the two men with his pistol pressed against Clint's head. Phillips was poised to take any measures necessary to restore order.

"Clint, there is a little boy laying in the grass because you let your hatred get the best of you. Don't make me exercise final justice right here, because in some sick way it's exactly what I want to do."

He pressed the barrel of his gun even firmer into the back of Clint's head. Somehow the sheriff's words touched something in Clint and he dropped the knife and raised his hands in surrender.

Sheriff Phillips handcuffed Clint and read him his rights, then jerked him to his feet. They had one more piece of business to wrap up before this night would be over. Brad directed the sheriff, with Clint in tow, to the location where he had left Zak and Jim after their earlier confrontation. The two men were dazed but conscious. The sheriff got them to their feet and walked the miserable lot of them back to the squad car.

32.

Ricky lay in a pool of blood, Marlena bent over him. She was in hysterics as she cradled him in her arms.

"Please don't die," she wailed over and over again.

Adam tried to calm her, but there was nothing he could say to ease her pain.

Hatred's ugly head had been reared again in this small town. This time the innocent victim was a child. Marlena struggled to comprehend these senseless acts of violence. How could people be so blind to their own pain, letting it go unchecked until everything in its path suffered, only to have it come full-circle and be laid at their own feet again? She couldn't help but believe this anger was just a mask for the fear people held deep within.

Adam was finally able to pull her loose from the small boy. Lance checked his vital signs. He looked up at Adam and said with urgency, "There isn't much, but his heart is still beating. We have to get him over to Doc's right away. I'm afraid to move him, but we have no choice."

"What do you need me to do?" Adam said.

They both looked down at Ricky, surveying his motionless body. Lance ripped a piece of material from his shirt and pressed it against the bullet wound in Ricky's side. The child was bleeding profusely and he knew the most important thing right now was to stop the bleeding. Marlena was still kneeling on the ground next to Ricky, sobbing. She continued quietly pleading to Ricky to stay alive.

"Please," she said, as she nervously rocked back and forth, "Please, Ricky, please hang in there. You can do it!"

Marlena's eyes were red and puffy, her pleading became a backdrop to Lance and Adam's efforts to get Ricky the medical attention he so desperately needed. Lance directed Adam to go to the squad car to get the flat board from the trunk. They would use it as a makeshift stretcher.

Adam ran to the car. Marlena moved closer to Ricky. Lovingly, she looked down at him and tenderly stroked his forehead, all the while murmuring words of comfort and encouragement, holding vigil over the fallen boy.

She moved aside as the two men gently slid Ricky onto the makeshift stretcher. They lifted him up and carried him over to the squad car. Carefully, they placed him across the backseat. Marlena slid in next to him to help keep his body stabilized on the stretcher. Lance instructed her to continue putting pressure on the wound. She held the cloth firmly against Ricky's side. Tears still rolling down her cheeks, she tried to infuse Ricky who was now unconcious, with every ounce of love she had.

Adam and Lance got into the front seat of the car. Adam immediately turned around to lend his support, both in stabilizing Ricky's body and telling him he would make it. He then reached a hand back and gently stroked Marlena's forehead.

"Marlena, he's going to be just fine. We'll get him to a doctor and he'll take care of him."

Marlena looked at Adam and tried to manage a smile. She felt comfort in his caring, but at this moment, Ricky was barely breathing. As unwavering as Marlena's optimism usually was, the situation looked bleak for the boy, and she was beginning to wear down.

Adam turned to Lance. "How far away are we?"

"Not far at all. We should be there in about five minutes."

They sped along, sirens and lights flashing. With every moment Ricky remained alive as they got closer to Dr. Hankin's clinic, his chances of surviving seemed a little bit better.

The car came to a screeching halt in front of the old mansion, now converted to a modest clinic. It also served as Dr. Hankin's living quarters so he would be nearby in emergencies such as this. Adam and Lance immediately exited the car and flung open the back doors to get the boy. With Adam pushing from one side and Lance pulling from the other, they slid him out of the backseat and clear of the car, gently setting him down until Adam could come around. Each one grabbed an end of the stretcher and carried him up the steps to the covered porch. Marlena was ahead of them, banging furiously on the door and calling for help. Lance motioned toward the after-hours call bell with his head. Marlena pushed and pushed the bell until she saw a light go on inside the building.

"Hold on, I'm coming."

It was Dr. Hankin's medical assistant, Gladys, who answered the door. Frantically, Marlena, Adam, and Lance all began speaking to her at the same time. "Please, get Dr. Hankin. This boy has been shot. He needs help."

The woman, dressed in physician's scrubs, was taken aback by the sight of the wounded boy. "Oh my god!" she exclaimed.

She quickly motioned for them to bring him in and follow her back to the examining room. As she lifted the cloth covering the bleeding bullet hole in Ricky's side, she shook her head and grimaced.

"Gladys, where is Dr. Hankin?" Lance asked.

"He's not here."

"Not here!" Marlena exclaimed.

"Yes, he left this morning for a two-day trip to visit relatives in Virginia. He commented that in twenty years of Blossom Festivals, he'd never treated anything worse than a scrape or a minor burn. He left me here to handle things."

"Well, can you handle this, Gladys?" Lance asked with concern.

"As a physician's assistant I am trained in how to stop or slow the bleeding and to give something for pain. That bullet has got to come out. I'm not qualified and I don't have the facility to handle something like this. I'm sorry. I'd like to try, but I'm afraid I would just make the situation worse.

"Gladys, do what you can," Lance said. "It'll be fine. How much time do we have with a wound like that?"

She thought for a moment as she began wrapping gauze around Ricky's body.

"He's in shock," she said. "I can slow the bleeding. But given his size and the chance for infection, if that bullet isn't properly taken out of him soon, we could lose him."

Lance, asking to use a telephone, was directed into the next room. He tried to locate the nearest qualified doctor to treat gunshot wounds. As Lance made his calls, Adam began to pace the floor. Occasionally he glanced toward Gladys, who was still applying the gauze dressing. Marlena continued to comfort the boy, speaking quietly to him and urging him to fight for his young life. Lance reentered the room looking defeated.

"What?" Adam said.

Lance looked at him with an expression of despair. "The nearest hospital with a trauma unit is in Shreveport," he said softly. "It's about two hours away and that's doing 80 miles an hour."

"Then what are we waiting for?" Marlena said, "Let's go. We aren't going to sit hear and just watch him die."

She turned to Gladys. "How much longer, Gladys?"

Gladys finished the last wrap of gauze. "All set. I'm going to give him a dose of morphine to help keep him comfortable on the way. And lose that board—you don't need it."

She administered the painkiller and motioned to Marlena she was finished.

"All right then, let's go," Marlena commanded as she scooped Ricky into her arms.

Lance was dazed.

"Lance we have one shot at saving this boy's life. Let's go, please!" Marlena said with urgency.

Adam and Lance followed Marlena as she moved swiftly toward the front door. Adam jumped ahead to open the door as she carried Ricky out to the car. Lance hustled ahead. He would have to drive like he had never driven before. They all piled into the car, with Marlena in the back holding onto Ricky for dear life.

Adam sat in the front staring out the window, his mind racing. Lance started the engine and sped off toward the highway to Shreveport. Just after Lance pulled away, Adam turned and said to him, "Turn around."

"What?" Lance said, as he continued speeding down the road.

"Yeah, Adam, what's going on?" Marlena said.

"Lance, turn the car around! Trust me," Adam said firmly.

Lance hit the brakes to slow down, made a U-turn, and headed in the opposite direction. "This had better be good!"

Adam wondered if it was the right thing to do. "Lance, head over to Sam's."

"Sam's?"

"Lance, remember when Mike talked to me about the condition of the Malibu? He said the engine was intact and there was only structural damage."

"You ain't gonna try and fly that crashed airplane, are you?" Lance said.

"It's our best shot at getting Ricky to a hospital. Shreveport is about 170 miles away. Even with some structural damage, I can get there in about thirty-five minutes, maybe less. Also, that 170 miles is measured by a road map. Roads are seldom built in straight lines, which is precisely how I'll be flying."

"Do you really believe you can fly your plane as it is?" Marlena said hopefully. "Is it safe?"

"It'll be a lot quicker than this car and a lot safer than some of the air buckets I've flown!"

Adam flashed a warm, confident smile that seemed to put Marlena at ease. Even Lance was grinning as he drove toward Sam's place. At that moment, Ricky let out a groan. It was the first sound he'd made since he'd been hit.

The squad car streaked down the road with lights and sirens blazing. They raced past the Thompsons' house and soon arrived at the long driveway leading to Sam's house. Partway down, Lance made a right turn, heading directly toward the downed aircraft.

Marlena gently rocked and comforted Ricky, telling him everything was going to be all right, occasionally looking up to see how close they were. Adam's stomach was filled with butterflies. Not only was this a risky proposition to begin with, but it was also his first attempt at flying since the crash. That alone made him ten times more anxious than any flight he'd ever made, including his first.

33.

The car stopped and Adam jumped out of the front passenger side. He bent over to the window of the backseat and yelled at Marlena to sit tight. Lance got out and followed him to the Malibu. As Adam searched his pockets, he realized he didn't have the keys. "Shit!"

"What's wrong?" Lance said, confused about what it could possibly be now.

"I don't have the goddamn keys. Shit! How could I be so stupid—Goddamn it!"

Lance thought for a second. "Does the lock work anything like a car door?"

Adam rubbed his head and answered hesitantly, "Well, I'm not sure. I suppose it would. In all my years of training we never studied door locks."

Lance trotted back to the car and returned with a jimmy. He began trying to figure out how the long, thin piece of metal could be slipped into the cabin door. The window was completely sealed. He tried sliding the jimmy in a crack running down the side between the door and the fuselage.

Precious seconds were ticking away. Adam, in his frustration, began pulling at the door handle in an attempt to force it open.

Just then, Lance excitedly announced, "I feel it. If I can just snag it I can—"

There was a loud click as the door unlocked. Adam tugged it open.

"Yes!" both men exclaimed simultaneously.

"Now, how you gonna get this thing started without a key?" Lance asked.

"Well, I think I left a spare ignition key taped to the rear seat. It's been so long, I can't remember."

He jumped in the rear section of the plane and began looking under the seats. He felt around under the chair at the rear—no luck. Then he looked under the two remaining seats, searching thoroughly along the legs where he normally would have taped the key. It wasn't there.

"Damnit!" he said in frustration. "It's not here."

"Is there such a thing as hot-wiring a plane?" Lance said, as he shrugged his shoulders.

Adam shook his head. "I could have sworn the key would be here," he said, rubbing his head.

Marlena approached the cabin, holding Ricky in her arms. She looked in at the two bewildered men. "How is it coming? We need to leave very soon. He's getting worse. The bleeding has picked up and he seems to be in a great deal of pain."

Adam and Lance looked down at Ricky, who was starting to cough a deathly-sounding cough. Adam also noticed a trickle of blood coming out the side of his mouth. Adam was determined to find the key and returned to searching as Lance explained the situation to Marlena. On hands and knees Adam frantically probed under the seats, again beginning with the second row of rear seats and working his way to the other two. He stopped for a moment, reviewing every possibility in his mind.

Could it have fallen on the floor in all the jostling the night of the crash? He began his investigation, first checking right under the seats, then behind them. He discovered a deep seam running along the floor behind the seats. He ran his fingers along the inside of it until he felt something—his eyes lit up.

"That's it!" he shouted joyfully.

He held the key up so Marlena and Lance could see it. They all smiled and again there was a surge of hope.

Adam directed them where to sit, assisting Marlena with Ricky and making sure he was in the most comfortable position as he fastened the seat belts around them. Lance informed them he needed to get back to help Sheriff Phillips. Adam asked him to make sure they got off the ground before he left, and he agreed.

Adam flipped on the master power switch to check the electrical systems. Everything seemed to be working. He went toward the cabin door to make a quick visual check of the plane before takeoff.

"What are you doing?" Marlena said.

"I need to do a quick walk through to make sure this baby will fly tonight."

Marlena looked a little discouraged.

Adam, sensing her doubt, smiled. "Don't worry, I'll get us there—in one piece."

She smiled nervously.

He hopped outside and began scanning the hull of the aircraft. He, too, became unsettled when he noticed a huge dent on the front end of the plane. He murmured to himself, "That'll create some drag."

He stood there for a moment studying the dent and the small cavity it created. There was no other chance for Ricky. He continued his walk around, tugging on the propeller to check its stability. Landing gear—check; ailerons and flaps—check; rear stabilitator, elevator, trim tabs, autopilot trims—check. He finished his walk around without the standard checklist. Tonight there wasn't time. He made sure to at least have all the essential items covered. He finished by checking the fuel and oil levels. The fuel was at about half, which gave him about two and a half hours. That should be plenty.

Everything seemed in order with the glaring exception of the dent in the craft's front right side. He turned to survey the field for the best stretch of potential runway. Any place he chose would be tricky because of having to take off without runway lights. The wind was blowing from the north, so he needed to try his best to find a way to take off in that direction.

He jogged into the field a short distance and knelt down to survey the ground. It was a little moist, but not too soft to stop him. He stood up and began running across the field, looking at the ground as he sprinted toward the trees at the far edge. He must have run about a half mile before he stopped. The surface was in pretty good condition. There weren't any gaping holes or impassable vegetation. He ran back to the plane, turning to look at the field once more, and said to himself, "This is it!"

He took a deep breath and patted the Malibu on its side, affectionately asking the craft to carry them as far as they needed to go. He walked briskly around to the cabin door and jumped inside. He looked at Marlena. "We're ready."

Lance had been waiting inside the cabin with Marlena and Ricky. It was time now for him to leave. He reached over to Adam and the two men shook hands.

"Good luck!" he said.

Adam nodded and Lance jumped out onto the ground. He closed the cabin door behind him and Adam locked the inside latch. He crawled into the pilot's seat and put on his headset. He switched on the electrical systems and set the instruments as accurately as he could. The fuel mixture was set and he put the throttle into starting position. Looking out his window to make sure Lance wasn't too close to the craft, he yelled, "Clear!" and turned the ignition switch.

The prop turned as the engine made a revolution but didn't start.

"Adam?" Marlena said.

He just ignored her, pumping the priming knob vigorously, then turning the switch once more. As he held the key in the on position and watched the prop turn, hope filled his heart. He continued to hold the key, almost torquing the head off of it. His fingers were tense. This baby had to start.

He pumped the throttle once, without luck. As he began to ease off the switch to try again, he heard the engine catch and turn over. The Malibu's engine roared as he again pumped the throttle. He turned and smiled at his passengers. "Just hold tight, Ricky. You're going to make it."

Marlena's face showed relief as she smiled down at the boy, still gently stroking his head. Adam looked out the window at Lance and gave him the thumbs-up. Lance smiled back and returned the gesture. Adam flipped on the strobe, position, and landing lights to give himself a clearer view of the field and began taxiing to the point he had selected as his runway. He spun the aircraft around so it was facing into the northerly winds. He looked down at the panel, grabbed the throttle, and pressed the brake so the plane wouldn't start rolling as he revved it up. As he slowly moved the throttle forward, the engine roared. He did one last check of the systems and everything was ready.

Once again, he looked back at Marlena and nodded. "Ready?"

She nodded affirmatively and Adam began to accelerate across the field. He focused straight ahead on the trees bordering the field as he applied full power. He gently pulled the yoke back as the plane rolled across the grass—just enough so the front wheel was pulled off the ground, in case anything had been missed in his quick survey. Having the front wheel off the ground would help keep the plane from grinding into the mud or dipping into any unleveled holes. With the nose high, he had to stretch his neck up to be able to see what was out ahead. The Malibu raced along the ground building speed, hopefully enough to clear the trees at the edge of the clearing.

As the trees grew closer, he pulled back hard on the yoke. The Malibu's gears began to slowly lift the plane off of the ground. Adam noticed that the medallion pressing against his chest felt like it was burning. He reached into his shirt and grabbed it, still in control of the aircraft.

Twenty-five, thirty-five, forty-five feet and they continued to climb, but a seventy-foot tree towered directly ahead. Thinking he wasn't going to clear it with altitude, Adam quickly made a sharp, sixty-degree bank to the right and pulled the yoke back. The Malibu veered sharply, just clipping a branch of the tree.

Marlena, looking on, exhaled as the plane leveled into a steady climb. Adam sank back in his seat and also gave a sigh of relief, still clenching the medallion with his right hand and flying with his left. Adam glanced back at Marlena and smiled. She smiled nervously, shaking her head in disbelief.

Adam leveled the plane at cruising altitude. "We'll reach Shreveport in about half an hour. I'm going to try and get some landing information."

He began his routine over the radio, trying to locate the best possible airport for a landing. There was only one airport whose terminal was open. He explained the situation, but no one could guarantee an ambulance would be available to get the boy to the hospital. Even if one was available, it would be another forty-five minutes to make it to the emergency room.

As they approached Shreveport the city lights became more distinct. Adam sat silently pondering the situation. He hadn't told Marlena the information he had just received over the radio.

"Marlena, do you know where the Shreveport hospital is?"

"It's on the northwest edge of town. Why?'"

"I need to fly over it."

"Why, Adam? You're wasting time. Ricky is losing so much blood back here. He's getting worse. Why aren't you just flying to the airport?"

"I'll explain later," he responded, not wanting to worry her further.

As they flew over the sparkling city lights, Adam turned northwest and headed for the edge of town.

"Marlena," he shouted over his shoulder, "do you think you can identify the hospital from the air?"

"Yeah, I think so," she said. "Adam, I don't know if you've lost your mind or what, but this boy is dying and you're doing some flyby of the hospital. Are you going to try and signal them or something? Why don't you tell me what you're doing? We are going to lose him."

Marlena was covered in blood and there was a steady stream of blood coming from Ricky's mouth as he continued to cough.

Adam shook his head. "Hang on, Ricky. We're almost there. We are going to get you there," Adam insisted.

Marlena was sobbing and clutching Ricky her hope fading fast. She could barely see through the tears that filled her eyes and streamed down her cheeks.

"Marlena, they can't guarantee we can get an ambulance at the airport. Even if we land and there is a taxi waiting for us, it's a forty-five-minute drive to the hospital."

"We won't make it," she said insistently.

"Right! Our only hope is to find a clearing by the hospital. A field, a parking lot, anything that will give us enough space to land."

"Oh my God, Adam."

"Do you trust me?"

"Yes."

"Do you believe in me?"

"More than you'll ever know!"

"Then let's find this hospital."

The Malibu was flying rough because of the airflow across the big dent in the airframe. It would occasionally dip twenty or thirty feet out of level flight. Marlena peered out her window trying to spot the hospital.

"There it is," she pointed. "To your right, ten o'clock."

Adam looked back, wondering where she'd picked up the pilot jargon.

"I watched a few war films with my dad when I was growing up," she said.

Somehow it lightened the mood and he smiled back at her as he began to set up for their descent. There didn't appear to be much open space around the hospital and the parking lot was pretty full. He made another slow, descending turn, and there it was. Across the street from the hospital was an empty parking lot, adjacent to an office complex. It seemed long enough, but the building next to it and the light poles would make things interesting.

He brought back the power and trimmed the plane to fly at eighty-five knots. Then he brought in full flaps and when he was down around eight hundred feet from the ground he pulled the power all the way back. He turned the aircraft so it was flying directly over the hospital and parallel to the office building next to the vacant parking lot. The office complex was right off his left wing tip. He had cleared the hospital and was about a quarter mile past it when he made a turn to the left. The Malibu was now descending at a rate that wasn't exactly comfortable for Marlena. She clutched Ricky tightly.

As the plane completed its turn, it was headed directly for the building. Adam had calculated his turn a fraction of a second too late. Only prayers could save him now. He continued to pull back on the yoke in order to clear the side of the building. As they grew closer, he again clutched the medallion hanging from his neck. The plane turned toward the parking lot. It was dangerously close to the building's concrete side.

As he turned to line up with the parking lot, Adam heard a loud, high-pitch screach as the aircraft's right wing scrapped against the wall. Marlena closed her eyes and screamed. Adam remained calm, holding the yoke with his left hand and the medallion with his right.

The tip of the right wing was torn away from the craft as Adam's turn lined him up with the parking lot. Looking out the front window, he was reminded of all the turns to final approach he had made before. Without much margin for error, he pulled back on the yoke to slow them down. Still seventy feet off of the ground, Adam was in full flare. Concerned about stalling the Malibu, he quickly put the plane in a slip by pressing the right rudder pedal all the way down and turning the yoke full left.

The plane cocked left and instantly dropped about forty-five feet. Just as he was straightening it out, the left wing grazed the ground. He again flared and the landing gear touched the ground. With the exception of the light post about seventy yards directly in front of them, their probability for a safe landing was looking good.

Adam slammed on the brakes, still holding the yoke as far back as he could and the craft began screeching to a stop. The question was if it would stop in time. Marlena closed her eyes, while Adam remained composed and intensely focused. Both of his feet were hammered onto the brakes and the yoke pulled back into his stomach. As they steadily closed in on the post, Adam felt he wouldn't make it, so he edged his right foot slightly off the brake to allow the plane to gradually turn left. It headed them just enough off center that the nose cleared as the Malibu ground to a halt with the right wing gently bumped up against the post. The plane creaked and moaned as it came to rest.

Adam shut off the power and jumped to the back to hug Marlena. She still had tears in her eyes. Her relief, however, was apparent. Adam helped Marlena up, took Ricky in his arms, and led them out of the Malibu. They raced across the parking lot and the street in front of the hospital.

The automatic doors to the emergency room parted, and both Marlena and Adam yelled for someone to help. A doctor quickly came to their aid, followed by two nurses wheeling a stretcher. The nurses took Ricky from Adam's arms. As they laid him on the stretcher, Marlena gave him one last caress on the shoulder before they wheeled him away. "Ricky, your going to be fine," she said.

She tried to follow.

The doctor looked at her and assured her. "Miss, he's in good hands now. It's best if you wait out here."

The nurse looked at her, reassuringly and nodded.

As they stood in the middle of the hallway watching Ricky being whisked away, Adam and Marlena collapsed into each other's arms. Whatever strength they had left they offered each other in the firmness of their embrace. Marlena wept quietly. It was out of their hands. Now only the will of a greater power could decide the fate of this boy who had touched them all so deeply.

34.

It was a bright, sunny afternoon at Bragg's Airfield on the outskirts of Eve. Adam was busy loading his belongings into the Malibu's baggage compartment. The aircraft looked impeccable, shining brilliantly in the sun's rays. All dents now gone, the plane was restored to the original luster it held that fateful day Adam took off from Atlanta's Peach County Airport.

"No detours this time, son," the voice called out from behind him.

It was Austin Thompson, there to wish him well as he continued on his journey.

Adam smiled. "Well, I sure hope not. This was the longest, most obnoxious layover I've ever experienced. I'll make sure not to plan a stopover in this town again."

"Well, it'll be sad times in these parts until you do. We'll miss you around here, Adam."

"Don't go getting soft on us, Austin Thompson," Marlena said as she walked up behind the two men, Sara at her side.

Sara made her way over to Adam and opened her arms to hug him. "Hurry back. This place is going to be dead without the two of you to add some excitement."

"Mom, we'll be back in three days," Marlena said "We're going to check out the airport in Friday Harbor to see if it's feasible, then Adam is going to bring me back here."

"Yeah, to pick up the rest of your things," Adam said affectionately.

Marlena looked over at him and smiled.

A loud siren sounded from a squad car as it drove onto the aircraft ramp. They turned and looked as the car approached. The sheriff pulled up alongside the group. As he and Lance got out, Lance proceeded to open the back door. Ricky slowly crawled out of the backseat. Their hearts went out to him as he struggled to move comfortably. His midsection was heavily bandaged and it was hard for him to maneuver. Marlena headed toward Ricky.

"You guys were forgettin' something. "Sheriff Phillips said,

Slowly and awkwardly, Ricky made his way to meet Marlena. He was holding a slip of paper in his hand. He spoke softly. "Ms. Thompson, you forgot your picture."

Ricky handed her the picture of Adam he had presented them with the night he was shot. You could hear a pin drop as everyone fell silent in their awe of the unwavering thoughtfulness and purity of Ricky's love.

Marlena kneeled down and hugged him.

Adam came to his side, saying, "Ricky, you hurry up and get healed, 'cause when I come back I'm gonna take you up in the Malibu and let you do some flying. Okay?"

Ricky gave his trademark smile as Adam knelt down and embraced him. Sheriff Phillips walked up to Adam and extended his hand.

"Son, I'm sorry for all the trouble you had here. It's in part my fault for allowing so many misdeeds to continue for so long. I'm truly sorry. I think things will start to get better around here with the help of a good newspaperman like Austin here."

He held up the day's issue of the paper containing a lengthy editorial on Eve's racial demise and how it was destroying the very fiber of the community.

"Adam, you're welcome in this town any time. If you let me know you're coming, I'll even pick you up from the airport. Good luck, son. I wish the best for you."

"Thank you, Sheriff. In the meantime, you'll probably be seeing quite a bit of me, since we'll be coming back every so often to visit the in-laws," Adam informed him, only half-jokingly.

Austin quickly picked up on it. "In-laws?"

They all laughed and said their final farewells.

Adam looked up at the sky. "Well, it looks like a nice thunderstorm is brewing. We better get a move on."

Marlena gave one last hug to her parents and Ricky and thanked the sheriff for all he had done, then walked toward the plane. Adam grabbed her hand and helped her step up into the cabin. Once he had his precious cargo on board, he turned and waved at the group.

"Wish us luck."

"Good luck," they all said in unison.

He made his way up the stairs into his prized and battle-hardened Piper, closing the cabin door behind him.

The propeller spun as the engine cranked up and began to roar. The plane slowly turned and taxied to the far end of the runway.

The group, now watching from a distance, awaited the successful takeoff as Adam revved the engine. The aircraft sat in place with the engine racing while a series of pre-takeoff systems checks were completed. A few moments later, the engine speed dropped to an idle.

Adam looked over at Marlena, gazing tenderly into her eyes. They were as beautiful as the first time he had looked into them. The absolute surrender of any doubts or fears that may have held Adam back in his life, reaffirmed the perfection of her being at his side. He sighed deeply, filled both with anxiousness and adoration for her.

"Well, are you ready for this?" he asked.

"I've been waiting for this my whole life!"

"I love you, Marlena. I would die for you."

She smiled. "I love you too, Adam."

Adam pulled onto the runway, lined up the airplane with the centerline, and stopped.

He paused. The thrill of approach and takeoff had been there ever since his first flight. He looked at the sky ahead, filled with high clouds.

"Let's do it," he said to Marlena, applying full power to the throttle. The craft began racing down the runway and the nimble Piper lifted off, heading directly toward the thunderstorm brewing ahead. Clutching the medallion that hung around his neck he said a silent prayer for both Sam and Lieutenant Jefferson.

Adam banked right, taking them away from the storm. He knew in his heart this storm wouldn't be his last, but that any storms he encountered could be overcome with faith, courage, and action. The faith he now drew upon was even more deeply rooted within. He had discovered the power of quieting one's mind, so often driven by doubt and fear, in order to access the wisdom of the voice within. It was from that place he had found true courage to act on what he had been directed to do.

The end